What better companion for a growing reader than a good book to enjoy and to read in from time to time.

Here is just such a volume, a collection of wonderful stories each stimulating and exciting and each pointing up one of life's great lessons by the action of the story and not by preaching.

These are stories by well known authors who understand the motivations and feelings of young people; stories that encourage reading while at the same time fostering honesty, integrity and general good conduct; stories that will be avidly read and re-read by girls and boys alike.

Everygirls
Companion

Everygirls Companion

Edited by
A. L. FURMAN

LANTERN PRESS, PUBLISHERS

NEW YORK, NEW YORK 10010

Library of Congress Catalog Number 68-11184

Published simultaneously in Canada by
George J. McLeod, Ltd. Toronto

MANUFACTURED IN THE UNITED STATES OF AMERICA

Contents

5

6 *Contents*

Everygirls Companion

Tarnished Dream

by ARLENE HALE

❁❁❁❁❁❁❁❁❁❁❁❁❁❁❁❁❁❁❁❁❁❁❁❁

Tarnished Dream

by ARLENE HALE

WILL YOU GO with me, Alice?" Ross asked.

Alice Evans nodded quickly before he could change his mind.

"I'd love to, Ross."

"Swell. I mean—I'll pick you up at eight. So long."

He backed away from her and collided with someone. His face turned pink. Alice turned to push the books into her locker with shaking hands. It couldn't have happened. Not really. This was just a dream, and soon she'd wake up to the harsh light of reality.

But the shrill ringing of the bell told her this was no dream. Ross Cole, the boy she had studied covertly in every class they shared, the boy who was probably as handsome as any other boy in school, this wonderful, wonderful Ross Cole had asked her, Alice Evans, for a date!

"Hey, Cy, what's the hurry?"

Alice winced at the nickname. Would they ever stop calling her that?

"I've got to get home, Marge," Alice answered. "See you tomorrow."

She longed to tell Marge about her date, in fact, she wanted to shout it from the roof tops, but she didn't. Everyone would look at her and wonder, "What does Ross Cole see in her?"

What did he see in her? Now that the first throes of excitement were behind her, she was faced with the same question.

The minute Alice reached home, she went to her room. She sat down before her mirror. Her hair was long and silky, turning up at the ends in soft curls. Her eyes were the kind of blue that she liked to think held untold depths. Oh, if only all of her were as good as her hair and eyes!

Her mother's reflection appeared in the mirror. "Home early, aren't you?"

"Hi, Mother."

"It seems to me you spend an awful lot of time in front of that mirror. Is my daughter getting vain?"

Mother's voice was light, as if to bypass the awful truth. That was a real laugh.

"Oh, Mother, why couldn't I have looked like *your* side of the house?"

Mother laughed uneasily.

"But, dear, you look like your father and me both. You're a very nice combination."

"That's a big fat lie!" Alice said vehemently.

"What kind of mood is this? I thought I heard you singing when you came in."

"Oh, Mother, you'd never guess what happened. Ross Cole asked me for a date tomorrow night."

"How nice!"

"Mother, what will I do? You know what I mean."

"He asked you, didn't he? Isn't that all that matters?"

Alice sighed. She felt like throwing something at the reflection in the mirror. Ross must have been out of his mind momentarily. Why, suddenly, had he asked her to go with him? He had never shown her the slightest interest before! And now . . .

"Stop your dreaming and come downstairs," Mother said. "I need some help in the kitchen."

"In a few minutes, Mother."

"Now stop worrying. Everything's going to be fine. Why do you insist on making so much of this?"

"It's pretty obvious, isn't it?" Alice snapped. "I'm sorry, Mother. I didn't mean to sound like such a grouch."

Mother slipped her arms around her neck and bent down to press her cheek against hers.

"You're very beautiful, Alice. Inside, where it counts."

Mother left, closing the door behind her. Beautiful! The word brought tears to Alice's eyes. If only she were! Even if she were pretty, or passably fair, she wouldn't complain. But to be like this—

She knew she'd make a mess of her date with Ross. It mattered so much. She'd be all tied up in knots inside. She'd say something foolish and before the night was over, Ross would be sick of his bargain, wondering what had ever possessed him to ask her in the first place; a girl with her kind of face! The dream she held so bright and warm in her heart was suddenly tarnished.

She was still brooding when she went down to help her mother. A few minutes later, Dad came. He hugged them both, his big face lighting up at the sight of them.

Later, at the table, Alice looked at her father and wondered again why she'd had to inherit his facial traits.

Later, in her room, Dad knocked on her door and poked his head in.

"I just heard the news. Ross Cole, huh? Nice boy."

She wished he'd go away. She couldn't bear to think about Ross. He was so perfect. She liked the way he walked, the strong straightness of his shoulders, the nice, good looks of him.

"Your mother says she has a hunch this is pretty special," Dad grinned. "Got a surprise for you."

He reached into his pocket and brought out his wallet. He took out some bills and pressed them into her hand with a wink.

"Buy a new dress tomorrow. A real pretty one. That boy's eyes will pop right out of his head."

Dad hugged her again. For a moment she buried her face against his shirt. He was so blind! He loved her so he didn't really see her as she was.

"You'll get a pretty one, won't you?" Dad asked. "Something blue maybe. I like you in blue."

"Yes, Dad. Something blue," she said, nearly choking on the words.

"That's my girl!"

She'd have to do it now, or he'd be terribly hurt.

Since the next day was Saturday, Alice slept late. When she awakened, her first thought was of Ross. Tonight he was coming! A thread of excitement ran through her again.

When she went shopping, the excitement lingered until she tried on her first dress. Then she found herself forced to look at herself in the mirror. She had to see herself as she really was. The fun and thrill went out of shopping. Almost methodically, she picked out a blue dress with a minimum of frills; one she was certain her father would like.

As she was leaving the store, she bumped into Aunt Clara. It couldn't have happened at a worse

time. Aunt Clara was fun, a bit bossy perhaps, but
ready to laugh at a drop of a hat. It was just at this
particular moment that Alice could take no pleasure
in looking at her. She knew that she bore a startling
resemblance to Aunt Clara. In fact, they had often
been taken for mother and daughter. If that should
happen now, it was almost certain to be the last
straw.

"Shopping, eh?" Aunt Clara's eyes twinkled. "Big
date?"

"Sort of," Alice said, wishing she could find some
polite way to say good-bye and leave at once.

"You're just the person I was hoping to see, Alice.
I've got to buy a new hat. Come with me and help
me pick it out."

"But Aunt Clara—"

"You've got hours to get ready for that date. Now
come along. Later, we'll have a snack."

Aunt Clara's snacks were monumental. Alice
loved them. Aunt Clara ordered the most peculiar
things when she went to a restaurant. She had
a kind of queenly air about her when she took a table. Alice envied her poise.

Aunt Clara tried on a dozen hats. Some of them
looked atrocious, others simply awful.

"Can't expect much with my kind of map, I suppose," Aunt Clara sighed.

"And I look just like you!" Alice growled.

Aunt Clara's eyebrows arched up and Alice nearly bit her tongue in two. How on earth had that slipped out?

"I dare say you have been blessed with the Evans family trait. I hated it as a girl, just as you must. But I soon learned it didn't really matter."

"Oh, Aunt Clara, how can you say a thing like that?"

"You'll find out. Now come on, let's do something else. I'm tired of looking at hats."

They went to a nearby cafe. Aunt Clara was well known there. They hadn't been at their table for five minutes before she had the waiters chuckling at her quick wit. Aunt Clara had a knack with people. She could wrap them around her little finger, even if she did have that one glaring thing wrong with her.

"I see your mood really is a glum one," Aunt Clara said. "Too bad. Glum moods are a waste of time. We have to take life as it comes to us, Alice."

Alice took a deep breath. Aunt Clara must have seen the frown flit across her face, for she laughed.

"Some old crepe hanger, aren't I? As soon as we finish here, I'm going home. Coming with me?"

"I expect I'd better get back home."

"The Wilson twins are to be there at three."

"Oh."

Aunt Clara laughed.

"I thought that would make a difference!"

The Wilson twins were special friends of Aunt Clara's. Two livelier youngsters couldn't be found. They were seven now and full of ginger. But Alice loved them nearly as much as Aunt Clara did.

When the twins arrived at Aunt Clara's house, everything was chaos. Alice was in the middle of all the activities, laughing so hard her sides hurt. The twins loved her. If they weren't playing tricks on her, they were climbing all over her lap, hugging her.

It didn't matter to them how she looked. She was completely at ease around them. It was only here at Aunt Clara's, playing with the twins, that she felt like a real person. Here, she could be just as she really was, not worried about someone calling her "Cy" or imagining someone was whispering about her behind her back. Here she was a new Alice Evans with no problems.

"I'm afraid I must go now," she said at last.

The twins shrieked in protest and clamored to keep her there. Aunt Clara smiled.

"You have a good time tonight, Alice, just like you've been having here."

Alice's happiness dwindled down to nothing. She shivered a little. How would she ever get through the evening without making him miserable and her too?

"You make it sound so easy, Aunt Clara."

"It is. Remember what I told you. It doesn't really matter."

Her words rang in Alice's ears all the way home. But it did matter, it did! No one knew how painfully it mattered!

She forced herself to get ready for Ross. She brushed her hair until it shone and noticed that two bright spots of color were in her cheeks. When she went downstairs, Dad looked up from his newspaper and whistled.

"Hey, that's all right. I hope Ross will appreciate you."

With effort, Alice bit down a sharp reply. Her hands were cold, and she felt shaky inside. She wished the night were over. Long before she was prepared for it, the doorbell rang. She went to answer it on legs that were as weak as water.

"Hi, Alice," Ross said.

"Hello."

Ross held the car door for her and helped her in. Her heart started hammering in an uncomfortable way. He was being awfully polite. She still couldn't understand how this had happened. She was with Ross Cole!

They went to a movie. She sat there in the darkened theatre and dared a glance now and then at Ross. His shoulder brushed hers as he leaned close

to whisper to her. She had the queerest feeling that
he was every bit as nervous as she was. That seemed
odd. A handsome boy like Ross Cole?

Later in the soda shop, Alice braced herself.
There were a lot of others there. Marge spotted her.

"Hi, Cy!"

The warmth rushed up from Alice's neck and
never stopped until it reached her hairline. How
could Marge be so rude? Must Ross be reminded of
that horrible nickname they had given her? Marge
came and slid in beside her without being invited.

"Hi, Jumbo," Marge said.

Alice looked up. Jumbo? Oh, yes, she'd heard the
kids call Ross that. She didn't know why; it seemed
to embarrass him, for he blushed. Why had Marge
barged in like this? Oh, everything was going
wrong, just as she had known it would. The dream
was tarnished for good.

"How are you, Marge?" Ross asked politely.

"I'll do. Good movie, wasn't it?"

"Very good," Ross nodded.

He was still red in the face. Marge turned to her.

"Say, Cyrano, where were you all day? I phoned
twice and you were gone both times."

"Marge—"

Alice kicked her under the table.

"Huh?" Marge asked unknowingly.

"Never mind!"

"What are you mad about?"

Alice refused to answer. Marge had said the hated name right out. Ross still looked embarrassed and didn't seem to be listening to what they were saying. Alice was thankful for that. Marge finally left the booth and went to join some others.

The sodas came. Ross was so nervous that he upset his. It ran all over the table top and Alice had to jump up in order to keep from getting soaked. Ross was so flustered he didn't know what to do. Everyone was laughing.

"Hey, Jumbo, what are you trying to do, drown the poor girl?"

The name again. Jumbo. How odd. Ross was of about medium height and weight. Why Jumbo? He wasn't that big.

"I'm sorry, Alice. What a mess. I-I don't know what's the matter with me. So blamed clumsy—"

"Never mind."

He was really ill at ease! This surprised Alice. She felt sorry for him, and she longed to help him. Talking might help. About something—anything. The Wilson twins. That was a good subject.

She told him about them and got so wrapped up in what she was saying that she forgot herself. She was as free and easy in talking as when she was with the youngsters. Ross leaned his chin in his hand, elbow on the table top and watched her.

"I've seen you at your aunt's with the twins. You had so much fun. I-I guess that's why I like you, Alice."

She swallowed hard.

"That's a funny thing to say."

"No, it isn't. We're sort of alike, Alice. I admit I'm tongue-tied around people. But since you seemed sort of shy too—"

He blushed again. For no reason at all, she felt bold. Perhaps it was the excitement of this date, this new knowledge that Ross was uneasy and nervous about it just as she was.

"Did you hear Marge call me that nickname, Ross?"

"Cyrano? Sure."

"Cyrano de Bergerac. I'm like him, aren't I? A big nose. It's a family trait of the Evans family. I hate it. It makes me so ugly!"

Ross stared with amazement at her outburst.

"Ugly? Don't be silly. I guess I always knew why they called you Cy, but I never agreed with them. I don't see—well, looks are only skin deep."

He broke off for a moment. Then he took a deep breath.

"After seeing you with the Wilson twins, well I just liked what I saw, that's all. You're different at school, though. I'm not very good at saying things, Alice."

She sighed.

"It doesn't really matter to you? I mean how I look?"

"Of course not! You've got something else, something the other girls don't have. Only thing is, I don't see it often enough. Don't hide your light under a bushel."

"Ross, you don't have to be nice to me, just because—"

"I'm not just being nice!" he insisted. "Look, I never talked this way to a girl before in my life. I-I never dared. I always thought they'd laugh at me if I tried."

It was Alice's turn to be puzzled. "Laugh at you?"

"We've both got a nickname, haven't we?"

"Jumbo?"

He nodded and she could tell he was fighting for control by the way he kept tearing a paper straw into tiny bits and wadding them in his fingers.

"Why do they call you that?" she asked.

"Jumbo's a common name for an elephant."

"I still don't see—"

"You're kidding. You mean you never noticed, never hooked it all up—"

"What are you talking about?"

"Well, I'll be!"

Then suddenly, he laughed. All his embarrassment and uneasiness was gone. He cupped his hands behind his ears and waggled them at her. Then she knew. She had never noticed before but they *were* rather large. Like her nose!

The whole picture came to her with a startling clarity. He worried about his big ears, she worried about her big nose. But she hadn't paid any attention to his ears or even noticed them for that matter. The same had been true of him.

He grinned and Alice knew that was going to be a date she would never forget.

"Come on, Alice. Let's go for a ride."

They went out into the night. The stars were shining. Ross' hand in hers seemed warm and friendly. She had an uncontrollable urge to laugh and have fun as she did when she was with the Wilson twins, for at this moment she truly felt beautiful. Aunt Clara was right. It didn't matter. Not really. Mother was right too. At this moment, she was beautiful—inside, if nowhere else.

She tugged at Ross' hand.

"Come on. I'll race you to the car."

Then she was off with a delighted shout and Ross followed. She could hear his laughter somewhere behind her. When he caught up with her, she liked the look in his eyes. She knew she hadn't seen the last of Ross Cole, and she was glad.

Everybody Is Somebody

by ETHELYN M. PARKINSON

Everybody Is Somebody

by ETHELYN M. PARKINSON

OUR HOME TOWN isn't very big, although Rummy
Goodwin thinks the sign is slightly misleading:

WELCOME TO DALE
Population 9,803
PLEASE DRIVE CAREFULLY
We Love Our Children

Rummy feels sure there are about twelve thousand people, if we counted noses. He started the
project, taking it street by street; but people didn't
cooperate. Some moved away, some had babies
after he had counted the family.

Rummy brought a map to Fords'. "Now," he told
us, "if you divide the town in fourths across here,
and across here, I got this quarter counted. There

were three thousand souls in it. So draw your own conclusions!"

"I like it small," Bill Edwards said. "Everybody sort of has a place in Dale. Everybody is somebody —even Sherry Walker, here."

Meaning me! "Words can't express my thanks," I told him. "So open big!"

As I fed him a spoonful of my sundae, Janie Conway hissed: "Who's that, who just came in?"

We all looked toward the front of the store.

Rummy whistled. "Who is that?"

Peter Sawyer smiled. "I can tell you all about it."

"It?" Rummy quipped. "Haven't you studied gender in grammar?"

"Well," Pete laughed. "Add five new citizens in the area you counted—the Claxtons. This gal is Celia. Goes to college."

"I hope Mike got his hair cut." I breathed. Mike's my college brother.

"And then," Pete said, "there's Thomasina. They call her Tommy. She's about twelve. And does she show promise."

"Twelve!" Rummy couldn't have looked more disgusted. "Promise of what?"

"Hope!" Pete smiled. "I'll clarify. There's another sister, Hope. She's our age. She's been sick and hasn't yet come outside in the nice, fresh, friendly Dale air. But after seeing samples, boy, have I been watching that Claxton door."

"If she's as charming as her sisters, I bet she left the love of her life somewhere," Janie laughed. "You boys won't stand a chance until he stops writing, or something."

Hope Claxton burst upon us in full glory on Monday. When she came in to register, Pete and I were in the school office picking up questionnaires for our respective study halls. I'll never forget how Pete's jaw dropped when she said, "I'm Hope Claxton?"

For some reason, she made a question of it.

She was simply unbelievable after seeing her sisters. They were blondes with gorgeous, shiny hair, quite long. Hope's hair was short, neither black nor brown. Just dark and limp. It was parted on the side and hung straight down a little below her ears. She wore glasses with dark frames and tinted lenses, but nobody would ever wonder about the color of her eyes anyway. Her skin was sallow. Her lipstick did nothing for her. Neither did her navy jumper outfit. She was almost fat.

Miss Lewis introduced Pete and me. "You remember Celia Claxton, who won that music award and played piano on TV last year?"

Pete snapped his fingers. "I knew that name rang a bell. You play piano, too?"

Without expression, Hope said, "Celia is our musician."

"Oh." Pete hitched. "Bet you're athletic. Tennis, maybe?"

"That's my younger sister."

"Oh. Well, hope you like Dale, Hope. Heh! Heh!" Pete hustled out with his questionnaires.

"Hope's program is the same as yours, Sharon," Miss Lewis told me.

"I'll be delighted to steer you," I offered.

Miss Lewis smiled. "You're in safe hands, Hope. Sharon knows everything."

There, I saw the first expression I had seen on Hope Claxton's face. High, high disdain.

We tried to like her. We waited a week before we huddled. Janie started it at Fords'. "That jealous Hope Claxton! When Sally played her flute solo in orchestra practice, Hope told us point blank that she wondered why Sally Andrews thought she was a soloist."

"Boy!" Pete said. "Hope sure is a washout for more reasons than the obvious. She downgrades everything and everybody."

"She sneered at Carolyn's hair." Janie said.

Rosemary leaned over. "She wondered which movie actress Pammy Schneider thinks she is, when Pammy wore that perfectly groovy plum-colored outfit."

I sighed. "It's too bad she's so jealous."

"You caught yours, too, Sherry," Bill laughed. "You've got the big-head, and you think you own the school."

"That's because I'm monitor for our study hall," I said at home that evening, as I related the story.

My brothers Mike, Paul, and Curt grinned. Mike winked at Paul. "If one's going to mix in politics. . . ."

Everybody laughed.

"Is Celia like her, Mike?" I asked.

"She's no more like Hope than she looks. Celia's already a candidate for campus sweetheart, Psi Chi choice."

"How about Thomasina, Curt?"

"Tommy?" Curt grinned. "Ask Paul about her."

Paul blushed furiously.

"No!" I exclaimed. "Paul, she's only twelve."

"Thirteen, next week," Paul said, "and acts fourteen. But don't go jumping to conclusions. All the guys like her."

"Well," I said, "not one boy likes Hope; and not one girl. She ought to do something about that jealous disposition."

"Maybe she can't," Mike said. "I suppose she suffers."

"Why not?" I demanded. "Jealousy only makes the jealous person unpopular. For instance, we're organizing a thing. We're calling it The Coffee House Club after the coffee houses they used to have in England. Of course, the kids drink milk; but we'll have bi-weekly breakfast meetings and discuss books on our list. It's extracurricular. Miss Groves will attend, and we can get some credit. And if we can help it, we're not inviting Hope Claxton! Absolutely nobody wants her."

They thought it over. Daddy spoke first. "That's one thing about you, Sharon. You've never been jealous."

I laughed. "Of just whom would I be jealous, and why? Some kids have things I don't have talent or something material or well . . ." I winked at Mother, "better looking brothers. But I have my own place. I'm secure. I wouldn't trade places with anyone I know. That's why I just can't understand a person like Hope."

"That adds up." Dad nodded.

"Adds up?" I said. "Daddy, what does that mean?"

"It means you've explained why you can't understand."

Right then the mail arrived. "Letter for you, Sherry." Curt sang out.

"Oh!" I breathed. "It's postmarked Webster. That means Cousin Rachel. And with a long weekend coming up."

It was a teachers' convention. "Trust Cousin Rachel to know," I said later in Fords', "and to invite me. She'll have tickets for everything in Webster. We'll eat at the nicest places. We'll shop for me."

Hope was there with her malted. For some reason, even though she was almost fat, she consumed a malted every day.

"Personally," she said, "I don't believe in loving one's relatives because they spend money on one."

There were gasps. "I think it's pretty nice, if you can get it," Rummy said. "Of course if you can't . . ." he shrugged. "You know what Brother Fox said, sitting under those grapes."

"That was telling her." Janie said, afterwards. "She crawled right into her shell."

"What do we do about Hope and the Coffee House Club?" Bill Edwards wondered.

"Nothing," Rummy said. "It's our privilege to set the standards for membership."

"She'd turn it down anyway, with one of her remarks," Janie said.

I wondered. By accident, I had walked to school with Hope several times and had made discoveries. She read the books that her sister Celia used at college. She read books I had seen on Mike's desk, works of people who were merely names to me—

Dostoevski, O'Neill, Euripides, and others. She
knew the stories of the operas.

Not making the Coffee House Club, she was
really going to miss out on something.

"It's entirely her own fault. Jealousy is a disgusting emotion," Janie said flatly.

"We're meeting Monday after school to or-
ganize," Rummy said. "Sherry, know who's going
to be president? You!"

"You're kidding!" I said.

"Straight goods," Pete told me. "Right, Janie?"

Janie hugged me. "It's unanimous."

Cousin Rachel met me at the bus station with her
big car. Everything about Cousin Rachel is big.
She's Daddy's second cousin by marriage. She's a
big woman with a big voice, a big house, a big
circle of friends, a big heart. Her big arms went
around me. I got a big kiss.

"My, I am glad to see you, kitten! You're even
prettier than last time. Now, if you're not
tired. . . ."

"I'm not tired, Cousin Rachel."

"Good! We'll stop at the house long enough to
get you unpacked, and we'll start down the town.
They have the sweetest suits at Whorfs'. I can't wait
to see you in one. I'm past suits. We'll have lunch
in Whorfs' dining room. They call it the Terrace

Room. Remember, they were starting it last time you were here? Well, it's something to behold. It's five stories up over the river. Now, I know Webster isn't New York, but it isn't Dale either."

On and on she talked and drove. She hit the high spots on her own curving drive and came to a halt in the carport.

"Cousin Rachel," I said, "I can hear your telephone."

A few minutes later she put the phone down and turned to me. Her face was stark with disappointment. "There went our weekend. It's my sister Cora. Dan's having an attack, and Cora wants me to come. If I don't and if this one should be really serious, Cora would never forgive me."

"I'll go right home, Cousin Rachel."

"Never! I won't hear of it." She was dialing. "Esther? Rachel. My brother-in-law's ailing. Yes, Dan. Probably ate a plum. Anyway, Cora's hysterical, and I'll have to go. Esther, how would you like to lock up that little apartment and move over here and chaperon the prettiest girl in town for a few days? I promised Sharon a weekend, and she's going to have it! Oh, you're an angel. Yes. You can drive me to the airport."

Cousin Esther is Cousin Rachel's cousin, a pretty, slender, very different lady, very nice—but not Cousin Rachel. She parked in Cousin Rachel's carport. "Now let's see, my dear. I believe we're to lunch at the Terrace Room and try to find a suit that will fit you."

"Cousin Esther," I said, "the telephone is ringing."

This message brought cries of delight. Cousin Esther's face shone. "We're going right back to the airport, my dear. You'd never guess who has flown in . . . Minka!"

Minka. Melinda Coppen. She was related to Cousin Rachel and to Cousin Esther. I had memories of seeing her, when I was small.

Cousin Esther gave me a run-down, as she drove. Minka was in international society, or almost that. She was smart, elegant, traveled. She spoke four languages fluently. She had gone skiing in Switzerland, had studied art in Paris, and had painted in England and Italy. She was going to have screen tests, probably.

We found her at the airport waiting amid smart bags. People were noticing her.

She smiled brightly. "Cousin Esther? It's so nice to see you!" She looked at me.

I said, "I'm Sherry. Sharon Walker."

"George's daughter," Cousin Esther explained.

Minka kissed me. "I remember meeting darling little cousins. Do you live here?"

"She came to visit." Cousin Esther fluttered toward the car. "And then Rachel got called away."

Minka sighed. "I would choose this time to feel like getting away from it all a few days. Don't let me interfere with any of your plans."

"My dear, I . . . we're so delighted." Cousin Esther carefully turned into Cousin Rachel's drive. "I'll let your mother's friends know you're here. You've not had lunch, Minka?"

"I had something on the plane."

"You'll want to change. I'll phone a few people."

First she phoned Mrs. Ferguson. "Yes, it's Arnold's Melinda. No, no. That was George's daughter you saw with Rachel. Yes, Minka's been in Europe and New York. She'll be here only until Saturday noon. Well, if you really want to, dear. I'll phone Eleanor. Yes, we haven't much time."

Cousin Esther phoned several ladies and asked each to phone several more. I looked up numbers for her. She was aquiver with excitement.

An afternoon tea evolved, and I was glad because, frankly, I was aquiver, too—with hunger. The luncheon at the Terrace Room had been completely forgotten. So of course, had the suit.

The tea was lovely. Minka was stunning, and the ladies crowded around her. Cousin Esther told them, "You should see her on a horse. She's

Gerard's granddaughter, you know. Remember how Gerard loved horses?"

A breakfast at the Riding Club got planned. "There'll be twenty-five," Cousin Esther told Mrs. Dunlap. "Wait! Twenty-six. George's daughter is here, too."

So it was up and to breakfast at the Riding Club, and there I committed a social blunder. Because I was last to enter the car I was the first to leave it. Three ladies rushed up and engulfed me, and Cousin Esther clucked like a nervous hen setting them straight.

"No, no! That's George's daughter. Here is Minka!"

One lady murmured, "Well, I was expecting a very charming young lady, and you certainly qualify."

"Thank you!" I smiled and stepped aside.

Minka got coaxed into a riding habit, because some young horsewomen wanted to photograph her on a horse.

Later there was scarcely time to dress for the little dinner Mrs. Trowbridge and her daughters gave at the Chatterbox. The *Clarion* sent a photographer and a girl reporter who was telling me she had met my brother Mike, when Cousin Esther fluttered up.

"Miss Keller, they're asking Minka about the screen tests and about her experiences in France.

You know, some of her paintings were almost accepted for a very important exhibit."

Miss Keller hurried over to Minka.

"I don't know about tonight," Cousin Esther sighed later. "Rachel got tickets for Theater Guild, and . . . oh, dear! We have only two."

I began, "Cousin Esther, I'm a little tired, and. . . ."

"Rachel wouldn't forgive me."

Mrs. Ackerman spoke up. "Herb and I were taking guests. They canceled out so we have two extra tickets. I'll make Sid . . . I mean, Sidney would love the play."

So I sat with Sid Ackerman who is eleven, if he's a day. During the love scenes, he told me about his baseball team and all the teams that his team clobbered.

Saturday morning Minka slept late. Cousin Esther and I whispered and tiptoed and rattled no dishes. I was starved when, at eleven, Minka appeared.

"I overslept. I mustn't miss my plane. I'm meeting these people in New York."

I helped hurry breakfast. We got Minka off and drove home. Cousin Esther took off her shoes.

"I'll do the dishes, Cousin Esther," I said, "and run the sweeper."

Running the sweeper, I murmured aloud, "almost this, almost that. Minka isn't special, herself. She hasn't really done a thing. It's just . . . circumstances that make her seem special."

Immediately I blushed. Hotly. *That one was worthy of Hope Claxton,* I thought. *And if Cousin Esther heard it. . . .*

I peeped. Cousin Esther was phoning someone —about Minka. She had not heard what I said.

But that night I lay awake a long time, thinking.

On Sunday just before I left, Cousin Rachel phoned. "Dan's fine. It was a Chinese dinner, this time. I'm sorry I missed you, honey. But there'll be another weekend. We'll make it count."

"This one counted," I said.

Monday morning, who should join me but Hope. She had a strange book under her arm and a chip on her shoulder. "I thought you'd stay in Webster, where everybody appreciates you," she said.

I laughed. "Well, I appreciate Dale. What's the book, Hope?"

She couldn't hide her surprise. "It's mythology. It's new. I'll have extra time in study hall. I don't see how some people dare leave their assignments for study hall. Especially that Rosemary Rondau, whose IQ isn't the highest."

I said lightly, "Rosie gets C's. That's average. May I see the book?"

Hope gasped and blushed a little with pleasure.

"It's not just Greek and Roman mythology. See? British legends. Eastern and Northern mythology. Other ancient religions—Egyptian included. It's absolutely fascinating."

"I like mythology," I said. "I'd like to know more."

"You do? You would?" Through the tinted spectacles she studied me. "I could loan you some books, if. . . ."

I was nodding. "I'd love it. I'll come over after school." I remembered. "Well, not right after school. But after supper?"

"I'll be home." Suddenly she laughed a funny little laugh. "I'm always home evenings. You know, I'm supposed to get out more and get my color back, but the sun still hurts my eyes."

After school the Coffee House Club got organized. I was elected president unanimously.

I appointed committees and announced, "Rummy, your membership committee will have a brief, important meeting now."

"Great!" Rummy smacked. "We've already drawn up this list of people to be invited. Here."

Bending over that list, I was thankful that in Dale everyone has a place, everyone is somebody, even "George's daughter!" I was thankful that I was secure, that I was somebody, that what I thought and said had some weight.

And that I had the courage, now, to throw that weight around.

I stood and smiled. "I have an announcement," I said. "I'll explain fully later. But right now I'm simply saying that I have good reasons for dropping a bombshell. So get set!" I took a deep breath. "Dear friends, you'll have to invite Hope Claxton to join, if you want me to be president; in fact, if you want me to belong to the Coffee House Club at all!"

Beth's Room

by BETTY FERM

Beth's Room

by BETTY FERM

THE MOMENT Mom stepped into the bedroom that
Saturday, I knew by her fussy, mother-hen look
that the letter she clutched in her hand was from
Beth. Only my sister Beth, with her flaming hair
and tempestuous ways, had ever been able to
visibly produce this overprotective instinct in my
self-contained mother. I laid my biology book on
the desk and waited.

"Jen," Mom began hesitantly, "Beth is flying
home this evening. She'll be here at seven o'clock."
Her worried glance traveled quickly about the room
—always Beth's room to her. "It will only be for a
few days, and I wondered if. . . ." She broke off,
aware of the closed look on my face.

It is my room now, I thought defiantly, staring
at the poppy-splashed wallpaper that shrieked of
Beth's taste, the oily stain in the rug that hadn't

made it through Beth's arty phase, Mopsy the good-luck doll Beth had nailed to the corner shelf, where she sat tightly wedged between my books.

Jen's room now, I insisted stubbornly. Jen, the serious one, two years younger than Beth, who had lived vicariously in the small room across the hall. Jen, who dreamed of being a nurse. Jen, who couldn't possibly be envious of anything as silly as the bursts of girlish laughter that echoed from the slumber parties in Beth's room; the ruffled clothes that always jammed her spacious closet; the steady pealing of the telephone through her high school days; the provocative giggling that punctuated her whispered conversations when the field finally narrowed down to Tommy Farrar, the most sought after catch in town.

Six months ago in June, on her nineteenth birthday, my exquisite white-satined sister had glided out of that room, down the stairs and into Tommy's waiting arms, to the triumphant strains of the "Wedding March." Dad had beamed with pride, Mom had furtively wiped at her eyes, and I had silently blessed the happy couple and made plans to move into Beth's room the following day. It was going to be Jen's turn now!

And the magic of the room had worked. It was less than two weeks later that I met Chris Devlin at County General Hospital where I volunteered as

an aide for the summer. Tall and lean and dedicated
to becoming a doctor, he was a sophomore at the
university; and his lab assistant's job in the summer
helped finance him through the winter months. Perhaps it was the light in his eyes when he talked of
healing the sick, perhaps it was meeting him in the
familiar hospital atmosphere, but for the first time
my throat didn't constrict with shyness on a date
and we easily bridged the gap of newness with
bonds of mutual interest.

Mom's words brought me back to the present.
"Of course, it's your room now," she placated. "But
it does hold so many memories for Beth. Be generous and let her stay here during her visit with us."

The way Beth had been generous with me, I
thought resentfully. But that wasn't exactly true.
As a matter of fact, Beth could be overgenerous
with a possession—but it had to be hers first. As
soon as a toy ceased to intrigue her or the newness
of a dress wore off, Beth was more than willing to
give it away.

Is this what you really fear, a voice inside
me whispered. *That Beth might be available once
again? Are you afraid to read the look in Chris's
eyes when he picks you up tonight and meets your
irresistible sister Beth for the first time.*

"Is . . . is something wrong between her and
Tommy?" I asked hesitantly. Beth had written me

twice in the first two months. An ecstatic postcard from the Caribbean where she and Tommy honeymooned, and a newsy letter from the Midwest when Tommy settled into his new engineering job. The letter bubbled with the excitement of the things they had brought up from the Islands, the search for the suitable apartment, and the decision as to what period furniture should go into it. Nothing about what Beth really felt. But I had seen the bulky letters that arrived every week for Mom in the last four months, and I suspected that she knew more.

Mom rubbed her palms together nervously. "Oh, I don't think so, Jen. Beth writes that Tommy is out of town now, and she just felt like seeing us all again. You know how Beth hates to be alone."

I nodded, not really believing the explanation. "I'll move back into my old room for a few days," I said, preferring that to the thought of being a third party at the tête-à-tête I knew would take place in his room between my mother and sister.

My mother smiled her thanks, and the puckered worry lines in her forehead eased a little. Even when it wasn't obvious, I could always feel Mom's concern for Beth, like a warm blanket whose shelter was being denied me.

Once, when I was small, I cried out to Mom that she was partial, that she loved Beth more than me.

Mom's face had crumpled with remorse as she folded her arms about me. "Jen, Jen . . . it isn't true," she cried, hugging me to her. "I love you both equally. It's just that in some ways your sister isn't as strong as you are. When you grow older, you'll understand."

I watched Mom click the door shut behind her now, thinking that I had grown older, but not wiser, because I still didn't understand. With a sigh, I crossed to the chest of drawers to remove some of my things.

It was funny about Beth not being able to be alone. Even as a little girl she had to have someone around. How many times I waited, longing to hear her quick footsteps patter toward my room, knowing that it was only for lack of something more exciting to do that she sought me out.

"Talk to me Jen," she'd plead, her blue eyes soft as a baby's. "It's so quiet in the house." And for just a few minutes I'd bask in the warmth of my sister's companionship . . . until the doorbell or the telephone rang and she was gone in a flash, trailing expectant breathless laughter through the hallway as she ran.

Constant activity, noise, and gaiety—this was the atmosphere Beth thrived in. And how I envied her. People frightened me—made me feel awkward. I was always sure I had said or done the wrong thing.

With boys I was tongue-tied. When they met me for the first time, the disappointment in their eyes was unmistakable. "Just a plain brown-haired kid without a bit of spark to her. Nothing like that red-headed sister of hers."

As time went on, I retreated more and more to my room where books and painting and music became my constant companions, transporting me into an engrossing, friendly world where I reigned supreme. "My daughter, the mole," Dad affectionately teased, as I burrowed deeper into the sanctuary I had created. I felt a smile tug at my lips as I thought of Dad . . . big masculine Dad, who found it necessary to go on hunting trips with his insurance office cronies every once in a while to escape the "machinations of a household full of females."

But Dad hadn't called me the mole in quite a while now. Not since I had moved into Beth's room, and especially not since Chris. For what had begun between Chris and me as a friendship had deepened into a warm, steady relationship we hadn't bothered to put a name to. And just as a bud tentatively begins to flower under the heat of the sun, so I could feel myself blossoming, softening, giving.

As the outer changes became apparent—the fashionable bobbing of my brown hair, the tailored clothes I chose designed to show off my figure, my subtle use of makeup—I could see how delighted Mom and Dad were. But it was the inner changes that mattered most to me and the infinitely precious gift of finding someone I was attracted to. And now Beth was coming home. I felt threatened . . . frightened that the flame which flickered so steadily for me in Chris' dark eyes could somehow be snuffed out.

It was Dad who brought Beth home from the airport that evening. In her fox-trimmed winter suit, she swept through our doorway like a Hollywood starlet. But the husky cry of "Mama!" was very real as she wrapped her arms about Mom. They stood for a minute in the downstairs hallway patting each other comfortingly, until Beth's moist blue eyes settled on me, then widened in surprise. She broke from Mom's embrace, and I could smell the expensive perfume as she leaned over to kiss me.

"Why, Jen, you've changed so. Pretty as can be —and that sexy knit dress. . . ."

"It's . . . it's good to see you Beth," I stammered self-consciously, all the old feelings sweeping over me. Beth had changed too, I thought but it was hard to explain exactly how. A trace of dissatisfaction in her face . . . a slight petulance to the set of her mouth.

"Jen has a dinner date in half an hour," Dad announced proudly. Beth's full lips rounded to a teasing "oh" of approval.

"I won't be able to spend any time with you tonight," I apologized. "How's Tommy?"

"Oh, he's fine." Beth said, bending to pick up her suitcase. "Sends his regards to all of you." Her eyes swept up our circular stairway. "I can't wait to see my room. I've missed it so!"

A conflict warred within me as Beth sped upstairs. I resented her casual "my room," as if nothing had changed—the prima donna returning to the scene of her triumph. Yet, I wished fervently that she would stay in that room and reminisce to her heart's content or at least long enough so I could avoid introducing her to Chris.

It looked as if fate was on my side when Chris arrived fifteen minutes early. But Mom and Dad insisted on drawing him into the living room for the social amenities they considered an important prelude to our dating. Framed in a wingchair, Chris looked handsome and serious with his long sensitive fingers resting easily on his knees, while I perched nervously on the edge of the couch. I listened absent-mindedly to Chris's discussion of the coming chemistry exams, Dad's hearty words of encouragement, and Mom's gracious urging of refreshments; but all my senses were straining to hear the first sound of a footstep on the stairway above.

"Jen's sister Beth arrived from the Midwest a little while ago," Mom said. "I was hoping she would come down to. . . ."

I rose quickly, unable to stand the suspense any longer. "Beth is probably too tired Mom," I interrupted, cueing Chris with a glance. "I think we'd better go now, or we'll be late."

If Chris was surprised at my obvious impatience, he gave no sign. Following me into the hallway, with Mom and Dad close behind, he shrugged into his coat and held mine up for me. With an imperceptible sigh of relief, I leaned back against him and half-turned my head, groping for my coat sleeve.

Another minute and we'd be out! Then I felt his body slowly stiffen and raising my head saw the expression close to awe that crossed his face as his eyes traveled upward toward the stairway. A feeling of illness came over me. I finished getting into my coat, then turned about, knowing whom I would see.

Dressed in a black velvet housecoat, with her hair brushed back from her face, Beth floated down those winding steps like a princess wearing a ball gown. The homage we paid to her beauty was the silence in which we watched. Beth broke the spell as she reached the bottom step.

"Hi," she greeted in her husky voice. "Isn't anyone going to introduce me?"

Dad cleared his throat. "Beth this is Chris Devlin, Jen's friend."

Beth smiled. "Nice to meet you."

"Same here," Chris said. I didn't bother to check the expression on his face as he stared at my sister. I had seen enough.

Mom slipped an arm around Beth's waist. "You came down just in time dear. Chris and Jen were about to leave."

"Well, then have a good time," Beth said, looking at Chris. "Hope I see you again soon."

"Same here," Chris mumbled, opening the door. Mom and Dad waved, I smiled stiffly, then we were outside. The cool air felt good against my hot cheeks.

We drove to our favorite restaurant, wood paneled and candle lit for atmosphere. I was quiet all through dinner, trying to ease the hurt within me by justifying Chris's reaction. Why had I expected his response to be any different from the dozens of others I had seen bowled over by Beth's loveliness? I wouldn't get annoyed if Chris openly gaped at a gorgeous movie star. Then why all the fuss? But I knew why—because it was my sister Beth who had come back to claim as her due the room, the center of attention, the adoration from men . . . all the things I had envied for so long from my small room.

And I had wanted Chris to be different. Wanted him to be impervious to Beth's beauty so he could be more mine. Unreasonable though it might be.

Chris tilted his head to one side, a concerned frown creasing his brow. "What's wrong, Jen? You've hardly said a word all evening."

"It's nothing," I muttered. "Just a slight headache."

He nodded sympathetically, then went on eating. It wasn't until he was halfway through dessert that he suddenly stared into space, shook his head wonderingly, and burst out with, "Boy, your sister is beautiful!"

My cake fork clattered to the table. How dare he rub it in!

Chris unconcernedly spooned another chunk of pie into his mouth, then continued. "But I kind of feel for the guy she's married to."

I stared at him. "Why?"

He thought a moment. "Well, from what I saw and the things you've told me, your sister, Beth, is like a queen bee who expects to be catered to. If everything doesn't revolve around her. . . ." He shrugged expressively. That kind of thing can be awful hard on a guy."

It took a few seconds for his words to sink in. "You mean you wouldn't want to marry a girl like Beth?"

He looked at me as if I had taken leave of my senses. "Jen, I'm going to be a doctor! Have you any idea what kind of a life most doctors lead?" He didn't wait for an answer. "Irregular hours, emergency calls, limited social life. The girl I marry has to put up with all that. She can't depend strictly on being with me. She has to have interests of her own, be able to make it alone at times." He reached across the table for my hand. "She's got to be someone special, Jen. Know what I mean?"

I nodded, too choked with happiness to speak. Our eyes caught and held for a long time.

Going home, we sat in a warm silence more eloquent than words. There was a special tenderness to the way Chris kissed me goodnight . . . as if he couldn't bear to let me go. I knew that something beautiful and lasting had happened between Chris and me that evening, and I floated up those winding stairs featherlight with joy.

A shaft of brightness pierced the darkened corridor and I realized that the door to Beth's room was ajar, even before I heard her voice drift out toward me like the plaintive wail of a child. She was obviously talking to Mom.

"Oh, it was all right in the beginning when every-

thing was new Mama, but now I can't find anything
to do there all day. It's bad enough when Tommy
is working in his office. At least then I can call him
up a few times a day. But when he goes out of town,
I can't stand it. You know I've never been much for
books and things, and the house is so empty and
quiet. . . ."

I tiptoed into my room and closed the door softly
behind me. For the first time in my life a feeling
akin to pity welled up inside me for Beth. Blessed
with all the outward social graces I lacked, my
beautiful sister had never bothered to develop the
intellect that might have given her the strength to
make it alone when she had to.

I moved out of Beth's room for good the next day,
knowing it had never really been mine. I was content at last to be Jen, surrounded by the books and
music and art work that had helped shape me into
the kind of girl Chris wanted to share his life with.
And somehow I knew that unlike Beth, when the
time came for me to leave this room, I would do so
without regrets, secure in the thought that I
was leaving nothing behind, but taking with me instead all the knowledge that I had acquired here.

Clean Sweep

by JOHN HENDERSON

Clean Sweep

by JOHN HENDERSON

I SUPPOSE I only had two problems about the Class Night Dance. That's THE dance of the year at Leesville Junior High.

A new dress.

Being asked.

By Fred Hilliard.

Guess that makes three problems, come to think of it. After all, other boys had already asked me, if you want to call "Hey Judy, wanna go to the dance?" an invitation.

Not that anybody in LJHS figured Fred Hilliard and Judy Burns—that's me—as going steady. Or anything remotely resembling that.

It's just that for the Class Night Dance, you don't show up with any old person that asks you. And Fred Hilliard had asked me to the Valentine

Valse and a couple of afternoon Beatle hops since then and—

Well, if he didn't ask me to the Big One, I knew I'd die. Simply curl up like those plastic gadgets in the supermarkets they set the soft drinks on.

One thing at a time, my father says. So I laid plans to get that new dress.

Midge Venturi and I spent a whole Saturday going from one store to another before I found exactly the right dress. It was a shimmering soft blue froth of a thing. Not too much of this, or that. Just right. And I already had shoes to match, and Midge said I could borrow her blue clutch bag.

So there was one problem solved.

Almost.

There was a big fat price tag on it that said, "$19.95."

"Don't worry," I said to Midge. "I haven't asked Daddy for a thing in months. He'll crash through. I just know he will."

He was away fishing when I got home that night, and somehow the next day, Sunday, didn't seem quite right.

I talked it over with my mother, and she halfway agreed the dress sounded right for me. She asked how short it was, then how low it was, and appeared satisfied when I described it.

"Try him Monday after supper," she said. "I'll

cook Polish sausage and sauerkraut." That's his favorite, as you may have figured.

But Daddy came home from the plant that afternoon looking as if he'd been slugged.

"They voted to strike," he said. "Don't know how long we'll be out."

I didn't even need to look at my mother.

There was still a month to go, so I let it ride. Maybe the strike would be settled in a hurry.

Meanwhile, back in LJHS, the other two problems were still brewing. Being asked. And by Fred Hilliard.

We're both graduates of the same sandbox, so I know better than to hint around with that character.

Oh, sure, he's sweet and kind and lovable. But rush him, you don't. He takes his own good independent time. If he feels like asking you to split a coke and pizza with him, he'll ask you. If he doesn't, there's no use trying any left-handed, swivel-shifting with him.

So I waited. And stalled off Norm and Pete when they asked me, or tried to sound me out if I'd say "Yes" if they did ask me.

A week after Dad went out on strike, Midge and I went back to the store where we'd seen The Dress. It was still there. As yummy as ever. And still $19.95.

That night I counted all the dimes and nickles

and pennies in my purses and dresser drawers and came up with the staggering sum of $1.13. My mother came in just as I stacked the last penny on the dresser.

She looked tired.

"Counting your wealth, Miss Miser?"

"Sure," I said. "I'm just rolling in it. I might even take a bath in it. A bird bath."

She laughed.

"I'm glad you can joke, dear. It—it looks like a long strike at the plant."

I knew. I'd heard the radio, too, and read the papers.

"What you're trying to say, Mom, is that the blue dress is out, right?"

"I'm sorry, dear," she said. "It's just too much at present. But I saw one at Marvin's . . ."

"I know," I said. "I saw it too."

We both sighed.

"It was like this when I was your age," my mother said. "I never quite got used to staying home when there were dances. There wasn't even baby-sitting to do then."

Baby-sitting—there were hardly any young couples in our neighborhood, so baby-sitting jobs were as scarce as middle-aged Beatle fans.

"You mean, if I could earn the money myself, you'd let me buy it?"

"Of course, dear. I saw the dress the other day, and I think you'd look beautiful in it."

"Oh, Mother!" I rose and hugged her. "Do you think, if I put something down on it, they'd hold it?"

"You could try," she said. "They're funny. I'll lend you enough to make five, then see what happens."

I could hardly breathe with excitement the next day in school. I was almost tempted to play hooky with Midge, for fear someone might buy the dress that day. But I stuck it out till three. Then Midge and I ran all the way downtown and into the Blue Dress store.

The saleslady in charge of the dress was definitely distant about the whole thing, but finally agreed to take it out of stock till the week before the dance.

That meant I had to dig up fifteen dollars in a hurry. Mom said she could wait for her four.

"Golly, Midge," I said, as we started for home, "isn't there anybody I could baby-sit for?"

She snapped her bubble gum before answering.

"The only family I can think of is the Mac-Mahons."

"Oh, no!"

They were Zero Minus in the notebook of every baby-sitter in town. No matter how badly they needed the money, the other kids always had a headache or homework, or both, if Mrs. Mac-Mahon telephoned to ask for a sitter.

A sitter? Better a squad of Marines and three psychiatrists to handle their little munsters. Take Joey.

By the neck, would be a good start. He was the only boy ever expelled from kindergarten on the first day of school. Then there was Letitia.

Letty had tied her third grade teacher to the piano and was starting a bonfire of "Dick and Jane" books under her feet when the principal and the fire department broke into the classroom.

In Leesville, they were regarded as the sheer nastiness champions of all time. The last time the MacMahons went out they had to hire the entire defensive backfield of the Leesville football team, and even then the boys phoned the police for help by nine o'clock.

And I was supposed to put my head into that lions' mouth or den?

"She pays well," said Midge. "Two dollars an hour."

Two—I gulped. If I could survive ten hours of MacMahonism, I'd have the dress paid up and to spare.

"I'll do it!" I said.

Midge looked at me as if I were a sky diver ready to do a Geronimo without a chute.

"You're crazy!" she said. "They don't even offer Blue Cross!"

"Never mind the Blue Cross, I want that blue dress."

When I phoned Mrs. MacMahon that evening, she jumped at my offer to sit.

"Why bless you!" she screeched. "I think the last movie my husband and I saw all the way through was *Gone With The Wind* before we were married. Come on over right away!"

"Uh, what are you paying, Mrs. MacMahon?" I asked. After all, there had to be some recompense for going into the snake pit.

"Two dollars an hour," she said. "And a two dollar bonus if we get to see the whole movie."

"It's a deal," I said. And hung up. For I had a plan.

"Good luck!" said my father, when I told him about it at supper. "Do you want me to stand by with my deer rifle?"

"Thanks, but I think I can manage."

When I opened the front door at MacMahons, I almost turned and walked out. Two different TV sets were blaring away full volume. Joey and Letitia were standing each other off, using overturned sofas as forts.

What's so unusual about that? How many parents

do you know who let their kids throw lighted fire-crackers at one another?

Mr. MacMahon and his wife were all ready to go, car keys in hand. They looked as eager to get out as lifers facing a parole board.

"Remember, we're a permissive family," said Mr. MacMahon. "The little darlings go to bed when they feel like it. Remember, no violence. Use reason and psychology."

Oh, brother!

The children paid no attention to their parents' departure, except that as soon as the door closed they began throwing their firecrackers at me.

"Hey, wait a minute, kids," I said. "I've got a new game for you to play."

They darted over toward me like barracudas.

"What is it, what is it?"

"It's called Indian Captive," I said.

"Whee!" they yelled. "What do we have to do?"

"First of all, we have to have some rope."

"I'll get mine," yelled Joey, and darted off toward the kitchen.

"No, use mine!" screeched Letty. She peeled off toward the cellar.

Joey soon returned, bearing a piece of rope tied into a real hangman's knot.

"I was saving it for later," he explained.

Letty hurried back with a long length of mason cord.

"Now what?"

"Well, first I tie you up," I said.

"Me, first!" screamed Letty.

"No, no me!" howled Joey.

"Please, you'll each get a turn," I said.

I fastened Joey's wrists together, and his ankles, and did the same with Letty. Then I anchored each child to a radiator, so they couldn't roll around.

"All ready?" I asked.

"Sure," they said. "Now what do we do?"

"First one to get untied, gets to tie me up!" I said. "Go!"

They both yelled with delight and anticipation. You should have seen the fiendish looks! Then they started working on their bonds.

I observed them carefully. I thought I'd done a pretty good job on tying them up. Joey was making definite progress, so I gave his wrists a few more turns with some nylon fishing line I'd thoughtfully brought along. There was some left over, so I used it on Letty. No sense in wasting it.

I'll bet Houdini himself couldn't have gotten out of the mess. They both screamed like real Indians when I added the nylon. They squirmed. They kicked. They twisted. Strange, the neighbors paid no attention.

Nor did I. As soon as I was sure the little dears were not going to burst the tie that binds, I lit into that house like a demon. Three hours later, when the parents were due home, it looked as if people lived there. I had straightened up the living room, washed the dishes, vacuum cleaned the rugs, and dusted. After all, I wanted Mrs. MacMahon to get her money's worth.

All this time Joey and Letty were whooping and hollering like Congolese rebels running over thumb tacks. But I found some cotton batting in the bathroom and went ahead with my work.

About ten minutes before the end of the movie, I approached them with The Deal.

"You go to bed quietly," I said, "and keep your mouth shut, and I won't tell anybody a baby-sitter outsmarted you."

Their reputations were at stake; they agreed, and I released them.

So when their folks came home a few minutes later, they nearly fainted.

The house was spic and span. No pools of blood anywhere. The children were in bed. I was in one piece.

"I don't know how you did it," stammered Mr. MacMahon. "But here's a ten spot. This has been the most wonderful evening of our married lives."

"Want to come back next Saturday?" asked Mrs. MacMahon.

"All right," I said.

Maybe I could work out another plan by then. For I knew Joey and Letty would be waiting for me. But the best laid plans of mice and MacMahons often go "kerflooie."

And to make life completely frustrating, a new boy came to school.

David Dodson was his name. Tall. Cool. Shoulders as broad as a—a garage door, almost.

But a woman-hater. Just about every girl at LJHS had tried in vain to get a date with him.

It was strictly fantasy with a capital "PH," I knew; but I found myself staring at the back of his head in algebra class and wishing he'd ask me to the Class Night Dance. For still no word from Fred.

But back to the MacMahons. On Saturday afternoon the phone rang. The mother of Joey and Letty was half in tears.

"Judy, did you ever have the mumps?" she asked.

"Why, no," I said. Which was the truth.

"Oh, dear," she said. "Willis and I wanted so badly to go out tonight, and Joey's down with the mumps. I don't suppose . . ."

"No, thank you, Mrs. MacMahon," I said.

So there I was. Five dollars to go. No dress. And no invitation, either.

Oh, Fred was making noises like he was starting to commence to think about asking someone. But for my money, he seemed to be awfully interested in helping Midge with her math and science homework.

A night or two before the deadline on the dress, Midge came over. We were setting each other's hair, as we usually did. I was backcombing when the second big idea hit me.

"Hey!" I yelled. "I've got it!"

"Ouch!" said Midge. "That's my hair, you've got."

"I know how I'm going to get the dress," I said.

"Fine, fine. But take it easy on my hair, okay?"

"That's what gave me the inspiration," I said. "I'm going to open a dog beauty salon."

"Thanks," said Midge. "Thanks a lot."

"No hard feelings," I said. "But I've had a lot of practice with Jock."

That's our West Highland terrier.

"There must be a lot of people in town willing to pay to have somebody else shampoo their dog, or trim him."

"Or give him a home permanent."

"Sure," I said. "Why not?"

So the next day—a Saturday—I put up a sign in front of our house, and the whole roof fell in!

My first customer was Mrs. Bradley. I mean, her dog. Gisele.

Gisele was one of those trembly, wet-eyed poodles that wouldn't harm a butterfly. At least according to Mrs. Bradley.

"She's become so nervous lately, I can't do a thing with the poor darling," she explained.

Talk about a tiger in the tank . . . I had a wild-cat in the wash tub. She snapped and bit and squirmed. I had on a sweat shirt and blue jeans, and by the time I finished bathing good old Gisele I was soaked from head to foot and the garage looked as if a soap suds hand grenade had gone off in it.

If it weren't for the two dollars Mrs. Bradley promised me, I think I'd have settled for bathing Gisele by squirting a fire hose on her. But finally it was done.

I handed her back to Mrs. Bradley, who bore her off in a pink baby blanket after giving me the money.

"There, there, don't cry," she said. So I was standing there, mad and splashed, about as cute as a wet dish towel when who should walk up toward the garage but Midge and Fred.

Midge was wearing a bright new summer dress. She was laughing at something Fred had said. Her hair looked terrific. No wonder. I was the one who set it!

"Oh, hi, Judy!" she said.

Get lost, I muttered to myself. But they came right up toward me and my dog laundry.

"How's business?" said Fred. I guess he meant to be friendly.

"Fine," I said. I was trying to do something with my hair when Midge dropped the bomb.

"Oh, Judy," she gurgled. "Guess what? Fred and I are going to the Class Night Dance."

Fred looked away. But I noticed his hand stayed glued to hers.

"Great," I said. "I hope you have a good time."

After all, a girl can't just come out and say exactly what she feels, can she?

"Well, we'll be seeing you," said Midge. They turned and walked out the driveway.

Really great, I thought. *Here I am. No dress. No invitation to the dance. And definitely not Fred Hilliard.* I was so mad and miserable and hurt I turned and stamped my foot. That was a mistake.

Splash! Most of me landed in the tub. My feet and arms were in the air, and I was half-blinded by soapy water.

I was trying to push myself up when I felt something wet slurping over my face.

"Max! Stop it!" said a deep voice.

Then I felt strong arms lifting me up out of the water, and a dry towel being pushed into my hands. When I got my face clear, there was David Dodson, the dreamy new boy in town. And he had with him the biggest, dirtiest, friendliest St. Bernard dog I'd ever seen in my life.

"You all right?" said David.

"Oh, sure," I said. "I was just testing to see if the water's hot enough."

He laughed, but somehow, not at me.

"Hey, a gal with a sense of humor. What do you charge to wash St. Bernards?"

"Three dollars."

"That's a lot of money."

"I know," I said. "It's a lot of dog."

He laughed again.

"Okay. I'll even help you."

Well, you know the old saying—they that wash dogs together go to dances together.

Even if Midge wouldn't let me borrow her clutch bag.

❂❀❂❀❂❀❂❀❂❀❂❀❂❀❂❀❂❀❂❀❂❀❂❀❂❀❂❀❂❀❂❀

A Matter of Communicating

by MADELINE TABLER

A *Matter of Communicating*

by MADELINE TABLER

MARY LYNN HAD been sixteen for a week, and she was sick of everything. She sat on the couch at the Allen's, her steady baby-sitting job, and studied her fingernails. This was the night, she decided. The night of all the last straws and the final curtains. This was the night she was going to the Coffee Cave.

She could still hear her parents, when she'd mentioned wanting to go there. "The Coffee Cave! I should say not!" her mother had cried. "I've heard some very unsavory things about that place," her father had pointed out.

Her boy friend, Rorey, had the same attitude. "Undesirable, M.L. Definitely off limits."

But she would show them. When the parents of her young charges returned, she would refuse a ride home. She'd just get on a bus and go to the Coffee Cave.

Conventional parents, conventional boy friend, everyone conforming, conforming. She was sick to death of it.

Before time to go, however, she went in and re-checked the sleeping Allen children.

When she had children of her own, she would communicate with them—ask them how they felt about things. She wouldn't run off to the PTA when her daughter wanted her new dress fitted.

She had wanted the dress for the party that evening. But her mother had replied with her usual, "Oh, Mary Lynn, you have a whole closet full of clothes to wear."

Mary Lynn went to the kitchen and dried the dishes. Then folded Mrs. Allen's clean laundry for her.

Mr. Allen's key turned in the lock just as the last diaper was tucked on the linen cupboard shelf. He came into the house giving Mary Lynn the impression, as always, that he was walking on unbroken eggs.

"Did the mites behave?" he whispered.

"Oh, yes, certainly." Mary Lynn spoke in a normal tone. They weren't going to awaken the babies.

"Good." Mrs. Allen opened her purse. She noticed the empty laundry basket. "Oh, thank you, dear girl. And you did the dishes, too." She handed Mary Lynn her sitter's fee. "Mr. Allen will drive you home."

"No." Mary Lynn felt her face flush. Her heart pumped faster and faster at the thought of what she was going to do. "No, I'll walk. I should walk more."

The Allens had arrived home later than they'd anticipated and were more in the mood to retire than to argue. So Mary Lynn walked.

A pang of regret struck her. When people trusted her, how could she plan deliberately to walk elsewhere than her supposed destination?

But her decision to go to the Coffee Cave had nothing to do with the Allens. The Allens weren't the important ones now. Her mother, who preferred the PTA to fitting Mary Lynn's dress. Her father, who was too busy with his business to talk to Mary Lynn. Her boy friend, Rorey, who wouldn't date on week nights, because he thought the team was more important than Mary Lynn.

She turned a corner and walked faster down the dark street to the bus stop. She sat by the window and gazed out as the bus left behind the large homes, then the smaller homes, along with much of her courage.

As she stepped off the bus, determination fought with regret. She tried to think. Then she heard the folk singer's voice wafting above the murmurings in the Coffee Cave. She stopped near the door, undecided now that she had come so far in her disobedience.

A boy appeared in the doorway. "Come on in, Chick." He was older than Mary Lynn. He grasped her arm just above the elbow.

"I don't know. . . ." Mary Lynn felt panic rising among her ribs. "I better not after all."

But the boy propelled her inside. "Don't be bashful." He murmured hello to several people and matter-of-factly put Mary Lynn on a chair at a table by the wall.

Her first visit to a coffee house! She breathed in a long shaky breath. Then breathed it out again. She wondered vaguely where the boy had disappeared to. And what she was going to do now that she was here.

"Talk to me. Tell me all your woes," sang the folk singer.

The boy returned abruptly and set a mug of steaming coffee in front of her. "Dig that."

She sniffed the misty scent above the cup—coffee with the smell of liquor.

"Cigarette?"

"No," Mary Lynn answered. "I. . . ."

"Don't smoke?"

Had he sounded scornful? No, more as if he

couldn't have cared less. She tried a sip of the potent coffee and wished she hadn't. "Uh—too hot," she whispered apologetically. "Is . . . isn't it against the law?"

"Coffee?"

"No. The . . . is it liquor? Well, whatever it is. Isn't that against the law?"

"Not very," he said.

How could anything be "not very" against the law? Mary Lynn gazed around her. At most of the tables lounged girls with long hair and boys who needed haircuts.

"You're frowning. What don't you approve of?" asked the boy at her table.

"Me? Nothing." The smoke stung Mary Lynn's eyes.

"You mean you don't approve of nothing, or you don't approve of anything?"

"I don't know. I guess I shouldn't have run away and come here."

The tears didn't come out of her eyes. They just waited there, along with those the smoke had caused.

The boy muttered, "Run away." Then he stood, grasped his mug in one hand, tucked his cigarettes in his pocket with the other, and glided away into the haze. Gone.

One shock followed close on another. Suddenly

uniformed officers burst through the door. Customers poured coffee on the floor. Some were intercepted halfway to the back door. The room became a shuffle, a swear word, a carousel, and finally it was no more.

Mary Lynn sat with long-haired girls in the police wagon, with seats at the sides. There were no handles on the inside of the doors.

A screen separated the girls from the two officers in the driving compartment.

Some of the girls acted nonchalant, crushing their cigarette butts beneath their shoe toes and sighing.

One pale red-haired girl who looked as if she had faded through long washing, held her head and repeated over and over, "No. Oh, no. Not again!"

Mary Lynn clutched her little purse to her stomach and blinked back the tears—which, she told herself, had been caused by the smoke.

Then she sat straighter. Now she had really done it. This would really show them. Maybe this was what was supposed to happen. She'd wanted to be different all right. What would they say now? What would the neighbors and the PTA and the business men say now? She'd really done it. Not only had she gone to the forbidden Coffee Cave, but she had also been carried off to jail or to the girls' detention house. She was frightened really, but still she felt triumphant. Her eyes dried. She found it easier to breathe.

Of course, what was different for her wasn't different for some of these girls, apparently. Like the one who kept saying, "Not again. Not again."

The police matron stood with her hands on her hips. Even her eyes looked plump. "I'm going to search you now."

"Search?" Mary Lynn rubbed her hands down the sides of her skirt and swallowed hard. "What for?"

The matron sighed as if she'd like to be kind. Then she cleared her throat. "Is this your first time with us, or are you trying to pull something?"

Mary Lynn was no longer sure how different she wanted to be. Or rather, she thought, from whom she wanted to be different. "I've never been here." Her hands clasped each other. "Could I call my father?"

The matron pursed her lips. When the matter had been given sufficient thought, she said, "We'll call your father. But before either of us leaves this room we're both going to know you aren't carrying any narcotics."

After the indignity, the matron put Mary Lynn in a small cell where she sat on the edge of the bunk and raged silently at herself and at her family which she blamed. Anger and fear took turns seething within her and chilling her completely. Hot tears seared her cheeks.

She had glimpsed the clock at the end of the hall coming in. Three o'clock in the morning!

Her parents were probably asleep. Rorey was asleep. It was a school night, and he would have been sleeping for a long time to be in shape for the big game.

"Mary Lynn, your father's here." A large woman stood by the door.

Mary Lynn blinked. She'd fallen asleep. Where was she? Oh! That was the matron.

She got up and smoothed her skirt. "Where?"

"Come with me." They walked down the hall; and as they turned the corner, Mary Lynn heard the no-not-again girl screaming. "Please. Please."

"What are they doing to her?" Mary Lynn gazed large-eyed at the matron.

"They aren't doing anything to her. She did it herself." The matron sounded cross. "She needs a fix."

Mary Lynn suddenly had the curious feeling she'd catapulted into the middle of a television show. Was this really happening? She had gone out to be different, but she had gotten herself into a jam. Mary Lynn's thoughts whirred on. She needs a fix. She rubbed a hand over her forehead.

In the visitor's room, they found her father pacing back and forth. For a moment Mary Lynn felt like running and throwing herself into his arms. Then the resentments welled up again. She stood still, clenching her fists by her sides.

"Sit here," the matron said, indicating a table with chairs. "You'll be able to tell your father how it happened."

The matron had set the stage and put the characters in their proper places. But Mary Lynn didn't know how to act. In a television play she might have said, "I wonder if this room's bugged." But it didn't even seem funny to her as the matron went out and closed the door.

"What happened?" Her father sounded stiff and formal. "What made you go to that place? After all we'd said about it."

The old resentments and frustrations that had gotten her in this predicament suddenly flooded up inside, and Mary Lynn let them out. Sarcasm she had never heard in her own voice before made it harsh. "Are you sure business isn't more important?"

"Mmmmm," murmured her father. "You mean you think it has been in the past?"

"Hasn't it?"

"I go to work to make money so you can have nice things—because you're my daughter and I love you."

The catch in her father's voice joggled a nerve way inside Mary Lynn. But there was no retreating. She raised her voice. "And Mother goes to the PTA because—because what?" she demanded. Suddenly the words began tumbling over and over each other in their haste to leave her lips. Words about the PTA, the dress, Rorey, everything being the same and the conforming and caring what other people thought all the time.

"You have got your signals mixed, haven't you!" Her father frowned, but he put his hand across the table and over Mary Lynn's. "Do you know why it was important for your mother to attend PTA the other night?"

"She wouldn't do my dress."

"You didn't really need your dress that night anyhow. Why should you have cared so much?"

"It's the principle of the thing!" Mary Lynn cried. "She thought they couldn't get along without her. What would people think if she didn't show up?" Mary Lynn jerked her hand away from her father's. Her voice rose shrilly.

"Is that why you ran off and got into all this trouble? To show you didn't care what people think?"

"We were talking about Mother and the principle of the thing." Mary Lynn sat stiffly. She would be cold, icy-voiced, stop her shouting.

"That's just why she went," her father said

calmly. "She went to uphold a principle she believed in. Not necessarily the popular one either. She believed that just because the Coffee Cave had such a bad reputation was no reason our area shouldn't have a gathering place such as Teen Club wanted to start."

Mary Lynn stared open-mouthed. "She was for the Teen Club?"

"With chaperoning."

"She wasn't going along with the herd?" Mary Lynn sat up straighter.

"And what about Rorey's principles? What did you expect him to do when he went out for the team?"

Mary Lynn interrupted. "How about us? Why didn't you say things like this before it was too late?" She burst into tears. "No, no! You only came because of what people. . . ."

The matron appeared in the doorway. "Are you taking the young lady with you?"

Mary Lynn's father stood and sighed sadly. "I don't know what to do. I don't think she wants to come."

His shoulders dropped as he went out the door.

Mary Lynn's bitter words popped, angrily echoing down the hall. "But what will people think?"

"I don't know," her father called back, "but they'll be able to hear that we're communicating!"

How can people be wrong and right at the same time? They can't, Mary Lynn decided. And they can't find out which is which without talking about it.

"Daddy, come back. I was wrong!" Mary Lynn shouted.

Her heart beat rapidly and her palms were as damp as her cheeks. She saw the glad look her father and the matron exchanged as he retraced his steps and returned to where Mary Lynn stood.

They stopped at the matron's desk, and Mary Lynn signed for the return of her purse.

"Do you want to wash your face and comb your hair before you go out?" the matron asked.

"No." Mary Lynn shook her head. "I just want to get home. I don't care what people think."

Walking beside her father, she took his hand as she'd done when she was a little girl. "Daddy," she said softly, "I think I'm going to like communicating."

Milly's Ideal

by BEVERLEY BAILEY

Milly's Ideal

by BEVERLEY BAILEY

MILLY TURNED slowly before the mirror and with a critical eye looked over her outfit. "I think I look pretty neat," she remarked to her reflection. The mirror cast back the likeness of a happy, healthy teen-ager. Dark hair, hazel eyes, and endearing personality were all reflected. No one would call her beautiful, but there was magnetism in her personality that made others want to be with her. She showed sincere interest in people and seemed to be perpetually happy.

She gave her image a sweet smile, a habit which had become as much a part of her grooming as combing her hair. She found it brightened her whole day to receive a big smile first thing in the morning—even if she did the smiling herself. Tonight she wanted to be especially gay; it was her first date with Danny.

Since Milly had just recently moved to Maxwell from Central City, she had not known Danny very long and was overwhelmed when this handsome and popular star athlete asked her for a date. She was unaware that he had some very definite ideas of the type of girl he wanted to go with. This was one reason he admired Milly—none of that silly stuff for him. "She's not always acting like she's trying to impress some male," Danny had told his mother.

Milly admired her reflection once more and then sat down to think things out with "Anna." She especially wanted things to be smooth on this all important first date.

Thinking things out with Anna consisted of thoughts such as: "Shall I wear nail polish? No, Anna never wore nail polish. If I want to start a conversation with that new boy, what would I say? Anna would probably ask him about that kooky little car he drives so proudly, then listen attentively and remember what he said. How in the world can I refuse that date with that funny Bobby Clane without hurting his feelings? Anna would be courteous and politely tell him she had other plans for the evening, even when her natural impulse would be to laugh in his face." And so it went—Anna always being the wise judge of what was right and proper for a teen-ager.

Sitting by the window and watching the evening darken, Milly thought back over the last couple of years to the time when she had first become interested in Anna. Anna wasn't really her name, but to Milly's way of thinking it fit her. And besides she couldn't even remember what the girl's real name was.

She was about three years older than Milly, a senior when Milly started Central City High. She was chic, vivacious, and constantly surrounded by a host of friends—mostly boys. She had grace and poise which awkward little Milly wanted to acquire so much; and to shy Milly, admiring from afar, Anna always seemed to be able to talk with no trouble at all.

With all these admirable characteristics, she had unknowingly become Milly's ideal. Milly still regretted that she had never had the courage to get acquainted with the girl. When you're a "country bumpkin" attending Central High, there are just some people you don't meet, socially or otherwise.

She remembered when she first started "consulting" Anna. Miss Gaines had asked her to do a special oral report in literature. *Oh, I just can't!* she had thought desperately, but she didn't dare refuse. That night, after failing miserably with Mom and Pop as an audience, she had had the thought, *How would Anna give this report?*

The next morning, armed with an idea and new-found confidence, she did an excellent job on the report. And that's how it was. With a lot of hard effort and the use of a vivid imagination on the art of imitation, Milly went about the task of self-improvement. Now two years later, she had poise, could converse well, had many friends and even the move to Maxwell hadn't gotten her down for long.

The first few days in Maxwell High she was afraid she couldn't go on without the real Anna there as a constant reminder. Now the worst was over and Danny had asked for a date.

Tonight had been no different. It was because of Anna that she hadn't worn too much make-up or a far-out hairdo. She sat deep in thought when two sharp rings of the doorbell brought her back to reality.

Milly made a wild dash for the door, but Anna slowed her down. She swung open the door, and Danny gave her the big roguish grin that made her heart skip. His smile was like an unexpected flood of sunshine in the middle of a storm.

He gave a low whistle. "Ooo-la-la." He tried hard not to laugh as he held out a handful of pitiful, wilted little flowers and said gallantly, "Only the best for milady."

Milly burst out laughing. "Nut! Come on in and meet my parents."

"What happens if they disapprove?" he asked with false seriousness.

"Just promise to have me home on time and you'll pass the P.A.T. (parents approval test)," Milly answered with a twinkling grin.

The introductions went smoothly and Milly felt sure that Danny had made a good first impression, mainly because he had remembered to ask what time they should be home. This was going to be a wonderful evening. *Anna, please, don't let me down,* Milly silently begged as they went out to the car.

As they left the house, he caught her hand and gave it a squeeze. "Gee, you look swell." He wasn't just being nice, he really meant it. He opened the car door, clicked his heels and said with a deep bow, "Your coach, Milady."

As he walked around to the other side, Milly took her little bouquet and closed the stems in the glove compartment so they drooped over the edge of the door.

As Danny got in, he spoke again, "I was afraid you'd be all decked out with goopy make-up and some wild hairdo."

"What's wrong with that?" asked Milly with mock indignation as she smiled to herself.

"Nothing, I suppose . . . if you're old enough. But why look twenty when you're only sixteen?"

"I'm seventeen!"

"OK then, seventeen. You look real neat the way you are."

Milly gave a little laugh and said an embarrassed thank you, and in her mind she gave Anna a great big, grateful hug.

She watched Danny as they drove on to the theater. I hope you're as nice as you look, she said silently.

They avoided the balcony crowd and sat in the last row downstairs. When he helped her take off her coat, he left his arm around her. She looked at him in the dim light and shook her head. (Anna would never approve of that.) She pointed to a couple about three rows ahead who had not come to see the movie, but to make a scene of their own.

"We might look like that to someone else," she whispered. His arm tightened around her for just a moment and then he withdrew it.

In a few minutes he whispered back, "Your hands cold?" He was grinning, and Milly was relieved to know she hadn't offended him.

"No."

After a slight pause, "Mine are," he whispered hopefully.

"Sit on them."

"Then I can't eat my popcorn."

Laughing, Milly gave him her hand. (Anna wouldn't object to that.)

Milly caught herself several times during the show watching the couple in front of her. She felt kind of sick; she'd never seen anyone act quite so badly. If they wanted to neck, that was their business, but why didn't they do it where others couldn't see them. *People who make such a public show of themselves must not have much self-respect, or the respect of anyone else,* Milly thought. Didn't they care about what others might think? Could they really care much for one another?

At the end of the first feature, Danny turned to Milly. He saw her watching the couple. "Pretty disgusting, huh?"

"I'll say!" Milly wrinkled her nose.

"What you say we go? The second feature is pretty corny."

"OK," Milly smiled gratefully.

At Danny's suggestion, they walked down the street to Sandy's for hamburgers and cokes. He started talking about various things, and Milly began to really enjoy the evening. The couple in the show were all but forgotten. They had disturbed Milly much more than she would have admitted to anyone.

Just as they were finishing, Danny nudged her

and nodded toward the mirror. She followed his gaze. Behind them, just going into a booth, was Anna and a young man. Really Anna! Milly's heart jumped.

Suddenly Danny's words seemed to scream in her ears as he said quietly, "Recognize them? They're the ones who sat ahead of us."

The bite of hamburger was like sawdust. "Are you sure?"

"Sure, I'm sure."

With tragic eyes she looked at Danny. "Please, let's get out of here." She slid off the stool.

Danny grabbed her arm. "Milly what's. . . ."

"Please, Danny," she pleaded. She pulled away and hurried outside. She walked toward the car, the hot tears about to fall. *For pity sake don't cry like a baby,* she thought wildly.

Danny ran up beside her, put out his hand and stopped her. Blocking her way and looking more than a little disgusted he demanded. "Don't tell me you're going to let those guys work you up that much!"

Milly could only shake her head. She tried to walk past, but he held her.

"Then what's wrong?" he sounded angry. "You look about to bawl!"

Without speaking, Milly pulled away and ran to the car, fighting the tears. He helped her in and slammed the door. He got in and slammed the other door. "Home?" he sounded sullen.

"Not yet." Her voice broke, and without looking at him, she knew he turned and glared at her.

He started the car with a jerk and a screech of tires. They rode for a few minutes in stony silence, and when he pulled up they were in the parking lot overlooking the lake. Milly would never have stopped here before because Anna would have objected. But now Anna and everything she had stood for had suddenly exploded.

The bright stars, night birds, and shimmering paths of lights on the lake all mocked her. Only the wilted, little flowers hung their heads and seemed to share her woe.

The girl had talked crudely and loudly to her companion, attracting the attention of everyone in the restaurant. So *THAT* was Milly's ideal!

By now her tears were under control. She looked away from the tantalizing lake and watched Danny's hand as his fingers drummed on the steering wheel. She would apologize and ask him to please take her home.

But control was all gone. The tears came in torrents and long hard sobs shook her body. She cried for several minutes, and Danny began to wonder just what kind of kook he'd gotten stuck with. He slid his arm around her—not knowing what else to do. She jerked away. She didn't want him or any other boy ever to touch her again. All she could think of was the way the couple in the show had looked to her. "You can take me home now," she said between sobs.

"Like heck I can! Your folks would have my scalp and demand to know what I'd done to their darling daughter." Milly stared at him. Gruffly he handed her his handkerchief. "All I can say is you sure must have led a very sheltered life if you let a couple that will act like that get you down."

"Oh, please, Danny, you don't understand."

"That's for sure! . . . Ah, Milly," he said, as he tried once more to comfort her.

"Don't touch me!"

He slid furiously across the seat and glared at the lake.

Milly composed herself, grateful for the handkerchief. When he spoke again, it was a little more gently.

"I'm sorry I made you cry, but I can't take you home like this. Your folks would wonder what kind of monster I turned out to be." He paused and after a deep breath went on. "Will you just kindly tell me now what all this guff is about?" He wasn't angry anymore, just downright worried.

Milly talked quietly, her breath coming in little shivers. She told him all about Anna and how although she had never been a close friend, she had relied upon Anna's example to help choose the right things to do. She explained that after she moved to Maxwell she still thought of Anna and decided to do things the way she felt Anna would do them. "That's why I didn't wear lots of makeup or a far-out hairdo. I just didn't figure she would."

"That all sounds fine, but what's it got to do with tonight?"

Milly bit her lip to help hold back the tears. "That was Anna in the show tonight. I didn't recognize her until she came into Sandy's."

"Yikes," Danny muttered.

"I feel that everything I've patterned my life after has suddenly blown up in my face. I've never told anyone else about this . . . I didn't want to be laughed at." She ended with a sob and a shiver.

"I'm not laughing." Danny suddenly felt sorry for Milly and really wanted to put his arm around her, but thought better of it. "You know though," he said slowly and thoughtfully, "you're really kind of lucky."

"Lucky?" She stared at him in disbelief.

"Now stop and think. Who let you down?" quizzed Danny. "It was that what's-her-name girl in the show." Warming to his subject he continued asking and answering his own questions. "But who helped you with your questions earlier today?

Anna. Now has Anna ever let you down? No. And really there's no reason why she should, because she's what you've made her. She isn't that cheap thing we saw tonight. Right?"

"I guess so." She smiled up at him.

"That's better," he said gently. "Does what I've said make sense?"

"Yes," she nodded. Then she added quietly. "I'm so glad you didn't laugh at me."

"It's no laughing matter as far as I can see. Everyone can use an ideal, and we all need to realize that we might be one for someone else. We get a big pep talk each season before we start playing. The coach warns us that being athletes, we have a lot of kids watching us that are wishing they could be like us. So we need to watch what kind of an example we set." Danny stopped and then another thought hit him.

"Hey, you know you really are lucky. Suppose you had gotten acquainted with this gal. With you thinking she was so great, you might have been so blind to her weak points that you would have turned out just like her. But now take your Anna—you and she are two pretty swell people."

"Thank you, Danny. Thank you for your patience and for talking to me the way you have." She smiled at him, her eyes still glistening from the recent tears. "I don't know what I'd have done if I'd been alone.

I guess I'll just pretend I didn't know the girl we saw tonight and keep on listening to Anna."

"That's my girl." He gave her one of those heart-skipping grins.

"I think you can take me home now without being afraid my folks will reach for your scalp," Milly said teasingly.

Danny laughed and checked his watch. "Yeah, we'll just about make it." Becoming very sober, he took her hand and held it in both of his. She didn't try to pull away. "Milly," he said quietly, "I feel this date was kind of jinxed. What you say we try again next week?"

"Oh, Danny, thank you. I couldn't blame you if you never wanted to go with me again."

Danny squeezed her hand and then headed for town.

Milly smiled happily. Life was going to be wonderful with a fellow like Danny and a girl like Milly's ideal.

The Practical Plan

by MARY WATTS

The Practical Plan

by MARY WATTS

I AM A DOG who has found his purpose in life. I
worry for the Gibson family. If Ginny loses her
algebra homework, if Mrs. Gibson finds ants in the
kitchen, or if a stranger comes to the door, faithful
Gus, the basset hound, is at hand to worry. Some
say that worry never accomplished anything. But
basset hounds learn from puppyhood to worry
creatively, and we try to follow up with a
practical plan of action in every case. This service
gives me a sense of personal worth which is often
missing in frivolous dogs such as that poodle down
the street. However, even a basset needs a vaca-
ton from the cares of the world at times.

I was sure on that first day of the vacation at the
lake cottage that a well-earned and lighthearted
holiday was at last to be mine. That afternoon, after
checking the dog food supply, I wandered down

109

to the edge of the lake to make sure that Ginny was all right. There seemed to be no need for worry. She was lying on the dock, oiled and simmering in the hot sun. So I crept under the dock to my cool hide-away which I remembered from last summer.

As usual, I allowed all four legs to let go at once, which caused me to land on the damp sand with a thud and then a groan of pure joy. I rolled over on my back and let my paws go limp against my chest. Suddenly I froze! Out of the tops of my eyes I saw a shadow slide slowly down over the top edge of the dock. A mop of dark hair appeared, followed by an upside-down pair of worried brown eyes. We were nose to nose before I gave a startled yelp and righted myself, as agilely as I was able.

"Gus," said the upside-down face, which was Ginny's, of course, "I heard you moaning and groaning under there. Come up on the dock and keep me company."

I rolled my eyes and sighed. A basset's work is never done, it seems. I worried Ginny through a serious illness and a long recovery. I worried with her until the doctors had given the all clear for a normal, active life. Then I had to worry the whole family down here to the cottage at Piney Lake for the summer.

Ginny's attention was fastened on the cottage next door. I put my head on her knee and watched

with her. There were some mysterious thumpings
and shoutings coming from the screened porch of
the cottage. As we watched, a lean, tall boy exploded through the screen door and galloped down
the beach. He churned into the water with a bellow.
Ginny's face lit up.

"Isn't he absolutely dreamy?"

The screen door had scarcely slammed after the
basketball player type, when a football player type,
with freckles and red hair, shot through it. As he
launched himself into Piney Lake, he gave a ban-
shee screech that set the hair quivering along my
spine.

While these two seemed to be trying to drown
each other in the lake, a slim, blond girl pranced
calmly down the beach and settled herself on the
sand.

Not one of them had looked over our way, but
my intuition told me that they knew Ginny was
there watching them. Ginny didn't get the same message.

"Gus, remember all those dreams I dreamed last
winter? I would be over here just like this and some
kids would come out, remember? I would smile and
say something clever and friendly and they would
invite me to come over. . . .

"What if they don't even notice me? How can I
get acquainted when I can't think of anything to

say or do even if they did notice me. I wish they would come over. I hope they don't. . . ."

This wasn't an ordinary kind of worry. It was close to panic. Now I am no expert on panic, but I know my duty as a basset. I realized that this was the time for action, if ever I was to have that vacation. A practical plan began to take form in my mind.

Ginny had turned over and was barbecuing her back. If she had been a dog, her ears would have been pricked up in the direction of the beach next door.

"Gussy," she whispered, "the dreamy one is Jerry and the redhead is Bob and the girl is Connie. I'd like to be friends with Connie. Do you think they've noticed that I'm over here?"

The practical plan was now ready for action. The answer to her question was to make doubly sure that the kids did know she was on the dock. With a silent apology to Ginny, I planted my icy cold nose into the middle of her sunburned back. The result was all I had hoped for—a shriek—audible for miles, shrill and definitely attention getting.

Ginny sat up.

"Gustave Basset Gibson! You come here this instant!"

I deemed it prudent to withdraw to the end of the dock until Ginny calmed down.

Now, I told myself, *those young people will have to notice Ginny.* I couldn't help wagging my tail in modest self-congratulation as we watched them pick their way along the path beside the cottage to a bright red canoe turned bottom side up.

Bob leaned against a tree and tipped his head to one side, "Why do you suppose she yelled like that?"

"Maybe she's been watching us, and when it suddenly dawned on her that she will have to be neighbors all summer with this nutty group, she simply fell apart. A natural thing to do." Jerry glanced over toward our dock, and I could feel Ginny's knee stiffen under my chin.

Connie gave a little shrug. "She doesn't even look at us. What do you bet she's stuck up?"

Ginny threw a stricken look in my direction. "Stuck up! If only they knew!" she whispered.

Something had gone wrong with my practical plan. Gloomily I watched the red canoe being hauled over the bank to the beach. I had probably spoiled Ginny's whole summer and my own vacation as well. And all because I was trying to help. I licked Ginny's hand.

Voices had risen again. We could hear advice being shouted by everyone to everyone else as they struggled to turn the canoe right side up at the edge of the water. It made a sandpaper sound as they slid it over the wet sand and into the water.

"Do you know how to paddle, Jerry?" asked Bob.

"I'll bet he does," Ginny murmured.

"Now don't you worry about a thing," grinned Jerry, "I'm an expert. We took the canoes out once while I was at camp last summer."

Bob wobbled uncertainly into the front of the canoe, trying to appear capable.

"We'll take her out and warm her up and then come back and give you a ride, Connie, O.K.?"

"Well, let's wait and see if you get back from this trip."

"You have no faith in us at all." Jerry waved a paddle over his head, climbed into the stern and pushed the canoe out into the water with the paddle. The canoe tipped madly and then swooped and bobbed as the boys started paddling.

Ginny giggled.

"They aren't terribly efficient paddlers, are they Gus? I bet you could do a better job. At least you would take it seriously."

She pulled my ear absently, as she watched the canoe travel in erratic circles. Once in awhile it tipped alarmingly as the boys practiced steering. They were whooping and laughing so loudly that the thought crossed my mind that perhaps they were showing off for the benefit of both girls on the shore. I could see the end of a rope making a ripple as it trailed behind the canoe.

Suddenly practical plan number two was born.

"Gus, what are you doing?" gasped Ginny making a grab for me. But I was too fast for her.

The water was pretty cold to jump into all at once like that off the end of the dock, but I was soon swimming in pursuit of the canoe. I didn't have to try to be quiet. The boys had gotten into a loud argument about which was the best side to paddle on and wouldn't have heard me, if I had been a moose.

I could hear Ginny as I swam. I thought at the time that she was cheering me on calling over and over, "Go, Gus, Go!" This spurred me on to my best effort. It was only later that I came to realize that she was probably saying, "No, Gus, No."

I had to approach from behind the canoe which took some doing since the canoe was spinning again.

As they came around once more, I put on a sudden spurt of speed and managed to reach the trailing rope with my teeth. I am naturally a strong swimmer, but this required all the strength I could muster.

Finally as I tugged on the rope, the canoe began to turn and then, little by little, I managed to pull it toward Ginny. I caught a glimpse of her, sitting upright on the dock with a hand at her cheek and a glazed look in her eyes. At the time, I had the impression that she was overcome with joy at my

brilliant strategy, but as I think about it now, I suspect that was not quite her reaction.

"Hey, Jerry. We're not going forward. Quit making it back up, now."

"Good grief, I'm not making it go back. The guy
in the front is supposed to do some of the work,
too." Jerry's face was getting red. "Just put your
paddle in the water the way I showed you and push
it back. . . ."

My teeth ground down on the rope and my neck
was getting tired. Those boys were going to notice
Ginny—or else.

The water under us was dark, but each time Jerry
pushed the paddle back, it made a light green swirl
of air bubbles not two inches from the end of my
nose.

"Jerry! Bob! Behind you . . . look behind you.
A sea serpent!"

Connie was dancing up and down at the edge of
the water. She had spotted me. Jerry heard her and
turned in his seat to look. Then everything happened
at once.

Jerry stood up in the canoe and twisted his body
to raise the paddle in the air. Just as the paddle
started to arc down toward me, his foot slipped in
the wet canoe. Bob turned to look back at this moment and unbalanced the canoe even more. The
paddles shot toward shore like missiles, the canoe

landed skidding upside down on the black water and the boys went in with twin mountains of spray. They came up sputtering.

I could tell that practical plan number two was never going to work. Jerry was pushing the canoe toward shore, and Bob had gone in pursuit of the paddles. I was surprised at how quickly, under stress, I was able to come up with practical plan number three.

Since Jerry seemed to be Ginny's favorite, I swam close to him and waited my chance until his bathing trunks were topside and I could take matters into my own teeth.

It certainly wasn't my fault that they were last year's trunks and already weakened by sun and water, or that a mouthful of trunks came off in my teeth. And then, if he hadn't resisted my gentle persuasive tugs on what was left of his trunks, I never would have had to growl at him and he never would have had to yell like that.

"Bob! Help! Help! The dog is attacking me. Quick, grab a paddle and hit him. Get away, get away . . . go on . . . ouch!"

Neither was it my fault that in the battle that followed, I just happened to be under water so that Bob hit Jerry instead of me with the paddle. Since it hit him on the head, he was groggy enough for me to rescue. Bob, in the meantime, had lost his hold on the paddle and had started off in pursuit. I decided to continue with practical plan number three as quickly as I could, and besides, I wished to be absent from that spot when the paddle got back.

Still holding doggedly to what was left of Jerry's trunks, I towed him the remaining short distance to our dock where I was able, with some pride, to dump him in the shallow water literally at Ginny's feet.

Well, there he sat, waist deep in the water, holding his head with one hand and his trunks with the other.

I must say that Ginny rose beautifully to the occasion, making my efforts on her behalf well worthwhile. Although what she said might not have been as clever as she had dreamed, at least it was friendly. She looked at that "absolutely dreamy" dripping boy, shivering in the water, gave him her most enchanting smile and said, "Hi. I'm Ginny."

"Good grief," sputtered Jerry, "is that all you can say to me after your crazy dog tried to drown me?"

"Oh, no. Gus saved your life after Bob hit you on the head with the paddle."

This, if you consider, was technically true.

"He did?" Jerry shook his head in a dazed way, as though he had just received another crack with the paddle.

"Yes, he did. How do you think you got way over here if Gus didn't bring you?"

"Well," Jerry was still a little bubbly from all that water.

"I thought maybe you came to my rescue since I notice my friends—my former friends—weren't much help."

Ginny looked down at the dock and followed an imaginary zigzag with a slim finger.

"As a matter of fact, I did want to come out and help, but I don't know how to swim."

"Good grief, you don't know how to swim? Really?" Jerry unfolded out of the water and then quite suddenly submerged. A hand could be seen like a pale fish under the water, groping for trunks. I could see that my day's work was still not quite done. With a sigh, I heaved myself off the dock once more. I picked up Ginny's large beach towel in my teeth and dragged it through the water to the shivering boy.

I had the impression that he wanted to hit me. But after all, you don't strike the heroic dog who just saved your life, especially if he belongs to a girl as cute as Ginny. Instead, he gave me a wet uncertain pat on the head and said weakly, "Thanks, Gus, I guess."

By the time the wet towel had concealed any gaps

in the swimming trunks, the canoe was beached and the other two walking over to our dock.

"Hey, Connie and Bob," called Jerry, "this is Ginny and she doesn't know how to swim."

"Hi, Ginny," Bob tipped his red head and grinned appreciatively, "I'll teach you how to swim, ahem, since I am the best swimmer in the group." He shined his fingernails on the imaginary lapel of his bare chest with the gesture of a boy who wants you to know that he knows he is bragging.

"You didn't do such a great job rescuing me from this sea monster." Jerry, I could tell, was beginning to remember what had happened. "I think Ginny would be safer if I taught her."

"It will take at least two experts to teach me how to swim," put in Ginny, "because I'm scared of the water, too."

"Hello, Ginny, I'm Connie." Connie finally managed to say. "I have been so lonesome for another girl around here. Your suit is simply fabulous. My girl friend has one something like it only the bow is on the hemline. What kind of sun tan oil are you using. I'm using new Brown and Serve. You want to try some? Do you play tennis? We have been looking for another player for doubles." Connie had to stop for breath.

I was proud of Ginny.

"I'm glad you came over after all," she said, "I

wanted to be friends right away, but I never can seem to think of what to say in order to get acquainted. I . . . I'm really not stuck up."

"Oh, I can tell you're not stuck up at all. I'm so sorry I said that. I didn't know a single thing about you, when I was talking about you. I had no right to say such a thing."

Ginny smiled at Connie and everything was marvelous. I joyously splashed everyone at once by shaking and wagging my tail at the same time.

"I'm trying the Terrific Tan Suntan Oil. Let's trade and then we can compare. I don't know how to play tennis. Will you teach me?" Ginny was saying.

"She doesn't know how to dance or even have fun with other kids, yet," I said. But, of course, they thought I was just groaning as I let my legs go all at once and thumped down on the dock for a nap. I rolled over on my back and let my paws go limp on my chest.

It's surprising how many practical plans there are that aren't so practical after all, I thought, *but if you are a basset, brave and true and never give up, you find one plan after awhile that makes creative worrying worthwhile.*

I closed my eyes and began my vacation.

Emily

by JUNE S. STRADER

Emily

by JUNE S. STRADER

SHE SAT on the front steps and closed her eyes. The air was sticky and quiet. If she sat very still and did not recognize the day, maybe it would pass her by. Maybe she would not have to do anything at all, just sit on the steps.

Emily heard the sprinkler in the yard, and the sound was sweet and familiar. She heard the soft whisper of bicycle tires sliding down the quiet street. And she heard a thin, tuneless whistle from the unseen rider.

If today had just never come, Emily thought. *Never come at all.*

She opened her eyes. She had to. Everything was the same. She had known it would be. Her legs still looked as white and as slippery and as fat as ever. The chalky flab of her calves looked as if it were about to dribble down over her ankle socks. Just like yesterday. Last week. Last year. Forever ago.

Emily did not have to look at her skirt. It was exactly like the others in her closet. All from the same pattern—only different material. She had once laughed to her cousin, Jessica, that her clothes were like Jello. "All the same, but in six delicious colors." Emily knew how to joke about being fat. She had been practicing for years and years.

She glanced down at her hands. Her long, slim hands. "The nicest thing about me," she mused. "Absolutely the very nicest." She was sixteen, and she wore a pale polish on her nails.

Emily thought about herself. Her hair was sandy and shiny and always clean. Her eyes were blue—really blue. She touched her face. Her features were nice and regular—and fat. "Just jolly old Crisco-fat in the can," she always told her friends. "Legs by Steinway, face by Bulova." She felt the tears begin, way down deep. It hurt to laugh, but it was better than showing her pain. Fat girls didn't have hearts. They had loud voices and deep guffaws. Fat girls didn't have many dates, either. Not many dates! Not any dates!

"I've got to get up and go in the house and get ready," she said aloud. "I can't put it off any longer."

She heard her brother, Joe, banging into the front

hall and up to the door. Joe was a year younger than she.

"Ah ha! here she is. Madame la Cow!" and he bowed low, as he opened the screen for her.

Emily rose, tried to smile graciously, and swept into the house. "Thank you, my good man."

Joe said, "Em, no fooling. You've got to hurry. It's almost time."

"I know. I'm going to dress now."

The class picnic was today. Now. And all of Emily's friends had dates to take them. At the last minute, her mother had suggested that Emily invite Joe.

"Oh, Mother! Nobody takes her own brother to a picnic."

"Honey, Joe would love to go," her mother had said. "And all the girls and boys like him. Go on and ask him." She had not said that a brother was better than no date at all. So Emily had invited Joe to go with her to the picnic.

Joe was taller than she. He wore glasses with black rims, and sometimes his voice wavered. His hair was a sandy brush. And Joe was thin, plain skinny.

"Em," Joe was saying now. "Em, are you going to wear shorts?"

"No, I'm going to wear a dress. I don't wear shorts

much anymore." She turned at the top of the stairs. "You go on and wear them, though. Everybody will have them on. Oh, and be sure to take your bathing suit."

Emily turned the corner and went into her room. Now that she was up and moving, she felt better. *I'll live through the day,* she said to herself. *I always do.*

She had already bathed, so she close a pale, blue shirtwaist dress to wear. When Emily began to be hard to fit in the stores, her mother had found a good dressmaker. She had warned Emily not to buy prints. "Mostly soft, pretty solids," she had said. "To go with your lovely skin and eyes."

When she had combed her hair and brushed her teeth, Emily dashed a light lipstick across her mouth and took four dollars in change from her jeweled piggy bank. She was ready to go.

"Mother, where are you?" she called. "You about ready to take us? Hey, Joe, you ready?"

"Yeah, Em! Be right there." Emily could tell Joe was pleased about going to the picnic. He wouldn't admit it ever, but she could tell.

"Oh, Emily, you look nice." Her mother watched her as she came down the steps. "You should wear blue all the time."

Emily knew that her mother worried about her.

She knew that her mother loved her, but sometimes it made Emily mad that her mother really didn't know how awful it was to be fat. She was blond and tall and graceful. She had never had a weight problem in her life. Emily's weight was not a problem to her, either. If Emily dieted, it would go away, given a little time. Her mother tried to understand about being fat, but she didn't. Nobody did.

Today, Emily wanted to grab her mother and never let go. She wanted to sit on her mother's lap and put her head under her mother's chin. She couldn't let her mother know, though. You didn't do that. When a girl was sixteen, she was grown. She didn't let her mother know when she was miserable.

When Joe was ready, they piled into the car— Emily and her mother in front, Joe in back. They all, very carefully, did not say that Emily was too fat to ride three in front.

The class had voted to have the picnic at Kessler's Lake, five miles from town. Emily's mother said brightly, "You will be right on time. Joe, try not to eat more than your share, and be nice to all the girls."

"Yes'm," Joe answered, from the back. "I'm always nice to everybody," he added, smugly.

He really is being nice, right now, Emily thought.

Any other time, he'd be teasing about how wide I am. She looked down at her loafers. She had just polished them.

Suddenly, they were at the lake. *Not yet.* Emily started wildly. *I'm not ready to be there yet.* And, then she was climbing out of the car with Joe.

"Bye, Mother. Thanks for the ride. Be sure and be back right at four."

"Bye. Have a grand day. Both of you." And her mother smiled and was gone.

"Hi, Em." Sue and Janet waved from the dock. They were very smart in their madras shorts and navy blouses. "Did you bring your bathing suit?"

Emily and Joe walked toward them. "Joe," Emily said. "Joe, you don't have to stay with me every minute. Just when we eat. Go on and have a good time."

"I will. Emily, I'm glad you asked me. You have a good time, too."

They were on the dock. Emily looked about her. Thank goodness everybody wasn't all paired off, yet.

"Hey, here comes Baby Blimp! Hi, Emily." Pete Hallet shouted as he climbed into the outboard motorboat which the class had permission to use. There had been a time when Emily had loved Pete Hallet. She had loved his loud, ringing voice and his bright red hair. There had been a time when Emily

Ann Clark would have put her head in a fire for Pete Hallet. And he had never known it. He said, now, "If you don't think you'll sink the ship, I'll take you around the lake." That loud, ringing voice was slightly rasping this year.

"Thanks, I'd love to. I won't sink that big boat. Just hold her tight, and I'll ease in." Emily grinned her best jolly-fat-girl grin and lowered herself awkwardly into the boat.

"Okay. Let's go," she said, and helped push away from the dock.

"How's your geometry, Pete?" she asked, when they were out on the lake.

"Oh, fine, now," he said. "I sure did appreciate all that help you gave me before exams. It was swell of you."

"I didn't do anything. You really knew it all the time. You just needed somebody to help you review."

She knew that everybody liked her. But, she knew too, that she was fat—actually, obese. Who wanted to date an obese girl? She couldn't even spend the night with other girls unless they had twin beds.

Pete rounded the lake once. "I'll get out now," Emily told him. She had seen him glancing toward the dock. She did not want to take advantage of his kindness. "Thanks for the ride. It was fun."

She climbed from the boat and joined the group

standing near the picnic tables. Somebody had brought a radio, and two couples had begun to dance. Emily loved to dance. She knew that she followed well and was light on her feet. Only a few boys ever asked her, and she nearly always embarrassed herself by appearing too grateful.

Today, she tried not to be interested. She tried to look away. Not to care.

"Emily, can we eat now?" She had not seen Joe all morning; now here he was.

"Sure, pretty soon. I just saw Mrs. Lester and Mr. Cheshire go down to the truck to start bringing the food. It'll be ready before long."

The day was nearly half gone. Emily ached inside. She was lonely. She wanted more than just to be thin. That really wasn't enough. She wanted to be herself, to be Emily Ann Clark. To have someone to talk to, who knew how she felt, inside. There was more to growing up than looking pretty and being the same size as everyone. She grinned at herself. "Of course, there's more; but right now, it would be nice just to be a perfect size ten."

And then, it was time to eat. The teachers had spread the picnic in neat orderly rows. Emily paid her three dollars to Anne Hillman, the class treasurer. She and Joe got in line with Pete.

"Hey, Emily, you better go to the end of the line! Leave some for the rest of us." Emily laughed. It didn't matter. Didn't it? Of course it did. But the thing was—the thing was not to let anybody know that it mattered. She hoped they'd see that she wasn't eating any bread.

After lunch, the couples began to drift toward the water. Joe had agreed to play shortstop in a softball game. Emily looked about for something, anything, to do.

"Hello, Emily. Having fun?" There was Mr. Cheshire, tall and tan, in his blue seersucker shirt.

"Yes, sir. Are you?" She knew that teachers didn't really have fun at eleventh-grade picnics.

"This is a nice bunch of kids," Mr. Cheshire said, pulling a cigarette from his pocket. "Want to sit down with me while I smoke?"

"Yes, sir." Emily didn't know what to say to him, but she was going to sit right there. She had always liked his blond hair and brown eyes. He was very tall and lithe, with strong, hard arms and hands. He had graduated from college only last year, and his students were impressed with his record as an all-state basketball player. Besides that, they liked him. He was fair with them; and he had a directness, which they admired.

Now, he asked, "Emily, what are you going to do about yourself?"

She crossed her arms over her stomach and hunched forward. She had always hoped that this position hid some of her flab. It really didn't, and she knew it. But, somehow, it gave her a sense of security to cover some of her fat this way.

"I mean, what are you going to do about being so fat!"

She stared at him.

"Look, Emily, I know this sounds cruel, and I expect it is—a little. But somebody has got to wake you up."

Emily could not believe what she was hearing. Was Mr. Cheshire actually talking out loud about her weight? She knew that her friends discussed it behind her back; but, nobody—nobody except her family and her doctor—had ever talked about it seriously with her.

"Mr. Cheshire, I've tried to go on diets. I just can't seem to lose. Maybe I'm supposed to be fat. There's nothing wrong with my glands. We've had that checked. Once, I stayed on a diet almost a month; and I lost eight pounds. But the minute I started eating, I gained them right back."

He smiled at her. "I know how hard it must be for you. I thought it might help to talk to someone, other than your family, and to someone who knows how it feels to be fat."

"How do you know?"

"I know because I was fat. How old are you, Emily? Fifteen?"

She felt her mouth shake. She must not cry. "Sixteen, last November."

"When I was your age, Emily, I was as fat, for a boy, as you are, for a girl. You'll go away to college year after next. You know you want to lose all this weight before then. You've got to."

She had heard only the beginning of what he said. "Mr. Cheshire, you weren't fat. Not really. Maybe you're exaggerating to yourself. You played basketball all four years in college."

He shook his head. "That was to prove myself to myself. Fat boys don't play basketball. A friend laughed at me once too often when I was nearly sixteen. That's when I decided to lose weight. I think you have to have an incentive, Emily; and that's why I'm talking to you this way. Don't be hurt. If I didn't care, I would have kept my mouth shut. You know that, don't you?"

"Yes, sir." She realized that she was sitting very straight. Her arms weren't crossed over her stomach. Hastily, she hugged herself again.

"How long did it take? How long?"

"It only took eight months, Emily. And a little sense about eating from then on. You've just got to make up your mind. That's all. That's the main thing, desire." He flipped his cigarette down toward the lake. "Your mother can help you diet. The doctor can help you. I can talk to you about it. But in the long run, Emily, it all comes back to you. You're the one who has to say no to potato chips and cokes and chocolate sundaes."

Emily looked at him. She looked at his long, gaunt legs stretched in front of him. "Mr. Cheshire, are you sure you're not fooling? Were you really fat?"

"Really fat. Not just chubby fat, but sure enough, honest to goodness, fat. Emily, growing up should be fun. I know it's a pretty lonely business, for everybody at times. That's part of the game, but it's fun, too."

"I have a good time," Emily said, weakly.

"I know. But are you having a good time now? Today? Seriously, are you? Was it fun asking Joe to bring you? Being afraid another boy would refuse?"

He had been fat. She knew now. The awful ache of terror that came with the fear of being refused. The hesitancy in asking.

"Emily, all this loud talking and joking about your weight. It's not really funny to you, is it?"

"No, sir. But it would be worse if I acted like I thought I was thin."

"I know. But you're such a nice girl. And you're pretty. You could be really good-looking."

"Thank you."

Mr. Cheshire's voice was firm.

"Don't thank me, Emily. I mean it. You're always selling yourself short. You are Emily Ann Clark;

and you are a fine worthwhile girl, who's going to lose some weight. And you must never again let me hear you sell yourself short."

Deep inside, Emily felt a rustle of hope. It could be done! She could do it. Suddenly, she felt as she had felt in the summer dusk when she was a little girl. And the wonderful play-outdoors-after-supper night was waiting for her. Only now, the whole world was outside, waiting. It was hers for the taking. She had only to want enough; and anything, anything at all was possible.

Emily smiled at Mr. Cheshire and stood up. "Mr. Cheshire, I'll make you a bet. This time next year, I'll be as thin as any girl in the senior class. Wait and see." He started to answer, and she interrupted him, laughing. "And just so you won't think I'm low-rating myself, I'll expect you to give me the very first dance at the prom next year."

He put his hand under her chin and held her face very still. "I'm not taking the bet, Emily. Because I'm betting the same way you are. I'm on your side. And I'll be proud if you will give me your first dance."

Emily felt a sudden, piercing thrust of self-consciousness. She thought, *What am I doing, standing here talking to a teacher about dancing with me? Have I gone kooky?*

"Run, now, Emily," Mr. Cheshire said. "Joe's

looking for you, and it's almost four. But, don't forget. I'm depending on you."

Her mind sang as she started down the hill. Mr. Cheshire. Emily Clark Cheshire. Emily and David Cheshire. David Cheshire's brown eyes had smiled at her. Emily straightened her shoulders. She began to run. This time next year, she would be as thin as any girl in the senior class. She would be. She knew it.

The Tide Runs In

by FRANCES DURLAND

The Tide Runs In

by FRANCES DURLAND

MAYBETH TRENT peered eagerly out of the window
as the train slowed for a stop at Ocean Grove. She
stood up, put on her new beige coat, and reached
up to pull down her heavy suitcase. Puffing she set
it beside her overnight case and the tennis racquet
her mother had insisted that she bring to camp. She
popped her pill box on her black curls and gave a
hasty swipe of lipstick across her pretty mouth.

Outside, she could see a small red brick station,
and behind it great pines and fires pointing towards
the vault of blue. Her heart was racing. She had
never in her fifteen years been away from home before. Now, for six weeks, she could forget her unhappy year at Englewood High, where her dad had
taken a job in the winter; could forget that she hadn't
made the Dramatics Club play; that no one really
liked her, and that she was much too fat! Surely at

141

camp no one would care. She pushed out of her mind the tall, lean figure of Stan and swallowed the sudden lump in her throat.

She bent down, dark eyes guilty, and shoved the big candy box under the seat. Now, why had she bought it, for she hadn't been hungry! She raised up, glanced at the petite girl two seats back who was also getting her things ready to get off. Other girls now were chatting excitedly, laughing together. Maybeth sat down, drawn into herself. Why couldn't she laugh and talk so easily with strangers? Instead, she always thought how fat she was!

Now they were crowding and shoving towards the end of the car. Maybeth moved down the corridor behind them, envying their easy comradeship.

Outside the train, she sniffed the sharp tang of salty air, her straight little nose crinkling. In the distance she could hear the steady boom of surf and a surge of excitement went through her. She would have fun, she simply had to, and she would stay on her diet and lose weight, she vowed.

She saw the bus waiting back of the depot, then met the smiling eyes of the young woman called Miss Gay. Answering her, she felt Miss Gay's warm kindness as she told all the girls to get into the bus.

"It takes us about half an hour to reach camp," she said in a cheerful voice.

Maybeth found herself seated beside the girl she had admired in the bus. She was a slim, pretty girl, with shiny red-gold hair, deep blue eyes shadowed by long curly lashes, and she wore her clothes with an air that Maybeth envied.

"I'm Priscilla Brynes," she said in a low attractive voice.

"I'm Maybeth Trent." Maybeth wished she didn't sound as if she was about to choke, and the hot color rushed into her round face. "I can hardly wait to get to camp," she added quickly.

"It will be fun," Priscilla answered. "I've never been to camp before," she shrugged slightly, "But the family decided that some outdoor activities would do me good." She laughed gaily. "I'm not much on sports. Except swimming," she added.

"Oh, I love to swim," Maybeth said enthusiastically.

Priscilla gave her a laughing glance, and said that Maybeth should be pretty good at it. "You should float," she said, not as if she meant to be unkind, but Maybeth felt something deep inside of her close up. Not that all her friends were unkind, but she was sick of hearing that it was hard to get clothes that looked right on her; tired of knowing that the boys avoided her at school parties. It wasn't fair! Some girls were like Priscilla, slim and petite, and *she* had to be fat!

The two girls chattered about camp until the bus drew up before the big yellow wood building, and they began to pile out. Maybeth clambered down too and stood looking about, her heart filling with happiness. The sound of surf was louder now, and back of the big yellow building she caught a glimpse of tents. Then they were filing up to the office, given tent assignments, and told all the rules.

She was in tent two, and she picked up her overnight case and started out to hunt for it. Miss Gay said their heavy luggage would be delivered by a cart. When Maybeth reached the tent, she found Priscilla was already hanging things up on the line which swung across the middle of the tent.

"Oh, I'm so glad you're going to be my roommate," she burst out. "I hoped and hoped, all the time on the train, that you would be."

"Good," Priscilla laughed lightly.

The tent had a wooden floor, and two small cots with heavy army blankets spread over them. A table at one end had two drawers for toothbrushes, combs, brushes, and other small articles. Miss Gay had told them there were hot showers in the main building and two or three tubs.

Both girls got into slacks and sweaters as soon as their suitcases arrived. Maybeth was sure that Priscilla kept eyeing her as she tried to change from her traveling outfit into her camp clothes. She glanced quickly at Priscilla, tying a bright blue scarf around the shoulders of her white blouse. She looked so lovely—Maybeth sighed—in dark blue slacks which fitted trimly over her slender hips. She glanced down self-consciously at herself. She never could look like anything but a baby elephant, she told herself with the old unhappy feelings.

"Let's go up on the porch where the whole gang will be," cried Priscilla and ran lightly away, while Maybeth puffed after her. Breathlessly she stopped to look out through the trees toward the sea, which lay blue and shimmering green, under a hot afternoon sun. A short distance off shore an old-fashioned four-masted schooner lay at anchor, and Maybeth thrilled to its beauty. Maybe someday she could swim out and board it! Then she hurried after Priscilla, who now was in the middle of a laughing group of girls, and was gaily telling some lively story.

Maybeth hovered at the edge of the group, uneasy, and wishing that she could think of something gay and witty to tell the group, to make them laugh as Priscilla was making them.

"You can just imagine me," she was saying, "in our last swimming contest, racing madly against this big girl, who puffed along like a porpoise, while little me just tried to stretch out as long as I could and get to the goal first. She was simply a whale."

Priscilla's blue eyes abruptly met Maybeth's

troubled glance, and the other girl flushed slightly. Then she went on gaily to tell about another time when she had won a race in swimming. Well, thought Maybeth, at least we will have fun swimming together.

"Girls," Miss Gay called out, "come into the assembly room and we'll go over our rules."

They filed in, some of the girls with their arms around each other, some laughing, some of the new girls a little shy and walking behind others. Maybeth followed Priscilla, who was already holding court, surrounded by an admiring group of younger girls. Priscilla might be sixteen or seventeen Maybeth decided.

They could swim three times a day, Miss Gay announced briefly, with her kind, warm smile. At six-thirty in the morning (she laughed as the chorus of pretended shivers went through the group) at eleven, and at three.

"And if there are very brave people," she smiled at them, "we might occasionally have an evening swim. And at the end of each week, we will have a water carnival in the pool. Most of you will want to practice there, but we will swim in the sea, too." She described the rest of the camp activities, and Maybeth listened breathlessly.

They would have handicraft, sings, hikes, picnics, and dramatic skits. At the end of camp, when it was open for families on the big day just before closing, they would put on a special performance in swimming and dramatics. Any who were interested could sign up.

"That's me all over," Priscilla tilted her bright head proudly. "I go in big for drama and swimming. I had the lead in our junior play," she added demurely.

"I love dramatics," Maybeth said quickly. "I'd love to act."

"You!" Priscilla's light laugh rippled out. "What part could you play?"

"Falstaff," one of the girls said with a jolly laugh and grinned good-naturedly at Maybeth. But there was nothing funny about it to her. She made her lips smile, but inside, it seemed as if the slow bleeding hurt of the last year had begun again. They didn't mean to hurt her, she reminded herself. They just never had been fat! She hadn't always been fat either, she thought achingly. But this year the more lonely she became, the more candy and cake she ate. For a minute she wondered again, why she didn't really want to, but she couldn't help it!

"Oh, I could manage." She tried to say it with the light airiness of Priscilla's gay manner, but it fell very flat because the girls just looked at her.

The next few days held so many exciting activities that Maybeth had no time to brood. Miss Gay and the other counselors kept things humming from the early morning dip to the last glow of the evening bonfire. Maybeth loved every minute of it, and while she often hung back, someone always dragged her into things.

She loved swimming in the clear blue pool, looking up at the sky, working up her form in swimming.

"Why go at it so hard?" Priscilla said lazily, one afternoon as they rested during quiet hour. "It's not such hard work."

"But I want to be just perfect," Maybeth tried to explain her longing to do something just perfectly. She wasn't even quite clear in her own mind why she felt she must excel in something.

The sea swimming was more exciting, dancing through the few breakers that came into their cove, where as a rule the water lay quiet. She loved it, and when she swam always looked longingly out at the anchored four-masted ship. What would it have been like to sail the seas in one of those, she often wondered.

Days glided by and before she knew it two whole weeks had slid by. Then one afternoon, Miss Gay called them all together, and her face was serious.

"Girls," she said, looking from one face to the other, "I don't like telling you this, but it is necessary." They looked up at her expectantly, and Maybeth's pulse leaped. "Someone has been sneaking into the camp during the night. The office funds were stolen from the locked drawer. Someone had obviously fiddled around the safe. I have reported it to the town authorities, and they are sending a gate guard. Probably whoever it was will not come again. But let's all be on the lookout for anything strange and report it immediately to me."

All the rest of the day there was a hum of excitement in camp in spite of the fact that Miss Gay had explained they must be calm and not let themselves imagine things. They hiked into town during the afternoon, and Maybeth bought a huge box of candy with her allowance. Back at camp, while the others were at the stunt meeting, she opened it up and sat on the edge of her bed stuffing one piece after another down her throat. Then she heard Priscilla coming and, in a guilty panic, shoved the box away back under the bed.

Night fell and with it a new silver moon rode across the sky. The water was black, and the surf seemed heavier than usual. When they went to bed, after camp fire, Maybeth lay and listened to it. Boom . . . you ought to leave that candy alone Boom . . . don't spoil two weeks of hard work swimming . . . Boom. Finally she fell asleep, when she felt someone shaking her. She sat up abruptly, her heart racing under her pajamas.

"Maybeth," Priscilla's pale frightened face glimmered into the gleam of her flashlight, "someone is sneaking around the tents. I heard him. I'm terribly scared," she whimpered. "What shall we do?"

"We ought to try to get up to the Main House and tell Miss Gay," Maybeth whispered back and started towards the open flap of the tent that faced the sea. She stopped, her throat tight, for across the dark expanse of night, lights winked out at sea. Frightened thoughts of spies and bombs raced through her excited mind, then she shook herself and told herself not to be silly.

"Oh, you don't dare go out and leave me," Priscilla's cold, wet hands dug into her arms. "I won't stay alone."

"Then come along," Maybeth looked at her in surprise, and bewilderment, for the poised, selfassured girl who was Priscilla seemed to have vanished and left instead a frightened, crying person quite unlike her.

"Suppose whoever it is grabbed us and carried us off?" she whispered.

"Don't be silly," Maybeth said flatly, surprised at herself. "We will listen, and we can make our way in the dark." She knew she too was scared, but she was thinking of all the sleeping girls in the many tents and of Miss Gay's words to keep calm and cool. Miss Gay could phone for help.

"I don't hear a thing," she said, standing very still

and listening with every part of her. She felt the goose flesh come out on her round arms, when again Priscilla grabbed her.

"Hear the footsteps," she whispered again, "they're coming this way." In the gleam of Maybeth's flashlight, her eyes were huge and blank with fear. Maybeth put out her flashlight, and stood waiting. It did seem as if she heard the faintest possible phff . . . phff of steps nearby. Her throat tightened and shivers ran down her spine. Then she heard nothing for a moment.

Then softly she began to laugh and pointed with a shaking finger to the open door of the tent, smothering her laughter, as she gazed at the dog that stood there, his tail wagging, his eyes gleaming.

Priscilla let out a smothered shriek. "What is it?" she begged.

"Nothing but a pooch." Maybeth walked towards the dog and held out the back of her hand for him to smell. With a final wiggle of delight, he came into the tent, flopped down beside her, and heaved a sigh.

"A dog!" gasped Priscilla, a look of chagrin on her pretty face, blue eyes confused and now looking a bit angry. "Well, it's a good thing you didn't go waking up Miss Gay," she said with asperity.

Maybeth looked at her in confusion.

"But you thought it was someone," she said accusingly, "and if the dog hadn't come, I'd have had to go."

"I hope you won't be silly enough to tell anyone about this." Priscilla crawled back into bed and pulled the covers up around her ears.

"I won't if you don't want me to," Maybeth said slowly, climbing back into her own bed. "But I think it's funny," she suddenly began to giggle. "And you were so scared. You even had me frightened."

"I fail to see anything funny about any of it," Priscilla's tones were muffled, "and it could have been someone. You know it could. We might have been killed."

Maybeth leaned down and patted the dog, which had curled up beside the bed. She couldn't go back to sleep for a long time, thinking of Priscilla. For almost three weeks she had thought Priscilla had everything a girl could want: a slim figure, a pretty face, attractive clothes, and poise and a sense of adventure that made her a leader. Now, she turned up to be a coward. It was very confusing!

Priscilla warned her, in the morning, as they hurriedly dressed for breakfast. "Don't say a word; I will fix you if you do," she said unpleasantly.

"OK."

"Girls, the guard caught the thief last night,"

Miss Gay confided, "so you don't need to worry."

Maybeth glanced at Priscilla, who shook her head violently and began to tell them how a dog had come to their tent in the night. Priscilla made it sound terribly funny and as if both of them had been scared. She had the whole group laughing by the time the yarn was finished. "And Maybeth was so funny when she was scared." She puffed out her cheeks and bunched herself together, trying to imitate Maybeth, and looked at her in triumph, as much as to say: now, you can't make your story stick.

"I wasn't scared that bad," Maybeth said heatedly. And I wasn't, she told herself stoutly. For the first time, she decided that maybe it was worse to be like Priscilla than to be fat. Priscilla had something wrong inside too, and she reached out and hurt others because of it. There was a faint murmur of laughter, then somehow, the crowd didn't respond to Priscilla as they usually did.

"Maybeth has a lot of grit," someone said unexpectedly, "you can see that, the way she sticks by her swimming."

"You're a swell swimmer, Maybeth," someone else said warmly.

And a third girl looked at her as if seeing her for the first time and said in pleased surprise: "Maybeth, you've lost a lot of weight. Working out?"

"You sure have," others cried and Maybeth felt a surprised glow of pleasure. She looked down at herself, aware for the first time that her slacks fitted loosely and that the fat little tummy wasn't nearly so bulging. Quietly she slipped back to the tent, and pulled out the big box of candy and hurried back to the crowd and handed it over. Somehow, it was easy now and she didn't mind saying:

"You eat it girls. I want you to have it."

The warm glow remained with her during the next few weeks as they got ready for the last big day. She and Priscilla were rivals now, each vying for the top honors in the Water Carnival.

The whole camp was seated on the rough bleachers around the pool waiting for the rehearsal—the last practice race. At last Priscilla and Maybeth were dashing through the pool in a neck to neck race—water splashing high. Almost at the finish Priscilla swerved slightly and her rapidly moving arm hit Maybeth square in the eyes as she turned to get a breath and she floundered, while Priscilla made the last few feet to the goal.

Rage tore through her and with it she lost all thought of self.

"You did that on purpose," she cornered Priscilla, who apologized and assured her that it was terribly unfortunate, that she had no idea Maybeth was so close.

"You do take up quite a bit of space you know," she said half laughingly.

That afternoon, Maybeth was still brooding, when they were all plunging about in the surf. It wasn't fair, but she had no real proof. She sat on the long dock, out by the deep water and stared out moodily at the weathered old ship anchored nearby.

"Challenge you to make it out there!" Maybeth stared down into Priscilla's wet and laughing face.

"We'll get too tired for our job tomorrow," Maybeth shook her head.

"Afraid?" Priscilla glinted at her. Then swam off. For a brief moment Maybeth fought a losing battle with her better judgment, then slid into the water, cleaving it with strong strokes, as she flung herself towards Priscilla. She would show Priscilla once and for all!

Suddenly she noticed that Priscilla was no longer pounding ahead, but was bobbing up and down like a cork, then she disappeared, came up, and flung up her arms.

"I'm coming, Priscilla," shouted Maybeth, heart pounding, and she forced herself through the water. "Keep your head." She tried to think of Miss Gay's quiet serenity, to remember the lifesaving training they had all had.

She snatched at Priscilla's red head, as she came

alongside of her, and pushed her reaching arms away. "Don't," she said firmly, and finally got Priscilla on her back and began to tow her in, talking as quietly as she could to the terrified girl, who had gasped out that she had a cramp and couldn't move.

Back on shore, breathless and exhausted, Maybeth was only vaguely aware of the girls who cheered her. She stumbled up the path and started towards the steps that led upward to the tent. Now that it was over, she was trembling.

Miss Gay hurried after her. Maybeth turned at her touch upon her arm.

"That was a splendid thing to do, Maybeth," her voice was soft and warm with approval. "And I'm proud of you. I've watched you these last weeks and I know it hasn't been easy. I wonder if you know how you've grown up?"

For the first time, in a long, long time, she didn't care whether she was fat or not. She didn't have to be fat! She could control that desire for sweets, if she had the courage to go and help Priscilla. It was all a form of courage. By the time she got home, she'd look exactly right. She wasn't going to be afraid of people anymore, she was going to be herself.

Special Invitation

by ADRIEN STOUTENBURG

Special Invitation

by ADRIEN STOUTENBURG

SHE HAD a feeling that the evening was too perfect to last, like a rainbow that would fade in a matter of minutes. The sunset with its twisted red ropes of cloud touched Brice's face as he opened the door for her and followed her across the flagstones. There was an air of expectancy about him, and then, as he pointed toward the driveway, Holly realized what it was.

"O Brice! It's beautiful!" She ran ahead to touch the sleek, black side of the convertible. "It's the final touch."

"Dad bought it yesterday," he said as he got in behind the steering wheel, "and I won out on the first chance to drive it." As he sent the car drifting between the two junipers that guarded the drive, he said: "Full moon due tonight too, for the wiener roast. Just as I ordered."

159

Yes, Holly thought. It would be. Life was like that for Brice Colbert. New cars, full moons, soft winds—all according to schedule. Not that Brice was smug about it. He just accepted them. She did too, though sometimes, like tonight, she couldn't help thinking how lucky she was. Again, as the car swept around the grassy curves, she had the sense of impermanence and of wanting to hold the evening and the date with Brice closer, as if the corners of twilight held some threat. The wind blew her dark, short curls back from her forehead and flapped the hem of her tweed skirt. "I feel like singing," she said.

"Go ahead," Brice laughed. "I'll start." He launched into a sea chanty with tenor gusto. She glanced at his clean-cut, bright profile, thinking: He's nice. I like him. I'm lucky he picked me for his steady this year.

Brice stopped singing suddenly. "This part of town gives me the creeps," he said, "but there's no other way to get to the picnic grounds."

She looked. The suburbs were gone, and the sunset had changed to an evil crimson that picked out all the worst features of the factory district, the used-car lots, the railroad yards. In the distance stood Brent High, a huge brick square bordered on one side by homes like hers and Brice's and on the other by homes like these—shacks, crowded apartment buildings, duplexes and four-plexes that seemed to lean on the wind for support. "A lot of the kids from Brent live here," she said, trying to imagine what it would be like, feeling the twilight pad forward like a great, silent animal with lavender eyes.

"Look," Brice said quietly, nodding his head toward a street corner where a secondhand clothing store and a tavern rubbed elbows. "There's Hugh Kittleson and his gang. Looking for trouble, I suppose."

The signal light flashed red, and Brice brought the car to a smooth stop, the tires sloshing in the water-gleaming gutter. Hugh and his gang stood scarcely ten feet away. Holly moistened her lips nervously and looked toward Brice. He was busy watching traffic. Hugh was in her art class. He was good too, better than she was, though he never seemed to be really interested. His paintings were cocky and tough, like him, and what he painted most were boxers. That was what he wanted to be, she guessed—a fighter.

"Hi," she called across at Hugh, smiling, but Hugh seemed not to hear. He stood with his legs straddled and his big thumbs hooked over his belt, a tall, glowering, black-haired boy with narrow dark eyes. The faint smile on his face wasn't friendly. The other faces weren't friendly either.

They were mocking, somehow and amused—as if there were something funny about her and Brice and the big coupe. She wished the light would change. She wished that Brice's father hadn't got the new car and that they were driving through Hugh's district in the old jalopy Brice had owned last summer.

"Better watch out you don't get any scratches on that buggy," Hugh called out to Brice.

Brice smiled. "I'm watching." His smile was not friendly either.

"Kind of muddy around here," Hugh said. "You wouldn't want to get any dirt on those nice new fenders." He glanced at a scrawny boy beside him and grinned.

The scrawny boy snickered and stooped down suddenly into the shadows. Holly saw the gleam of tin and heard the sucking sound. In a flash she knew what was coming. She stared straight ahead, waiting, as the car moved forward.

It came with a marvelous directness, the muddy water from the tin water gun splatting against the car. Several dirty drops trickled down her cheek.

"Why, you!" Brice shouted, whirling around in the seat. "I ought to get out and—"

"Please, Brice," she said. "Let's just get away from here."

He drove with one hand while he wiped his

face with his handkerchief. "Too many of them, and I'm no Joe Louis," he admitted. "But, boy! I'd sure like to see Hugh get what's coming to him! He's the worst kid in school. How he hasn't happened to be expelled before now is beyond me. Remember the time he and his gang put the salt in the water the water boy carried out to the squad last fall?"

She remembered. Her brother, Dick, had been team captain. Everybody knew that Hugh and his gang had been guilty, but it wasn't so easy to prove.

"Somebody will really beat him up someday," Brice went on. "That'll teach him."

"Maybe," she said. She wasn't sure. Her aunt worked in a settlement house and from what Holly had heard boys in districts like this one often got beatings.

Brice shrugged. "Well, no use letting Hugh Kittleson spoil our evening. There's that moon I mentioned."

It came up glowing and huge behind the smokestacks of a foundry and then, as they came out into the open country, glimmered across trees and water. Around a bend in the river a fire flickered. Another moment and Holly could see the individual figures of the picnic group and hear the music from Glen Andrews' portable radio.

"Look at the plutocrat!" Glen, a robust boy in

boots and breeches, hailed as Brice parked. He patted the sleek hood, and there was no resentment or bitter envy in his face. The rest of the group crowded around enthusiastically before finally drifting away to cut sticks for the wieners.

As Holly stood beside Cora Smith, a wiener crackling on the end of her forked stick, she thought: Why does Hugh want to throw mud on us, and put salt in the team's water pail, and make sneering remarks all the time? Maybe he thought we were slumming. He could be a good artist, but he doesn't seem to care. He could be nice, but he wants to be mean.

Hugh Kittleson nice? There wasn't any reason for thinking so, and she marveled that she had even thought it.

Later, as they sat around the dwindling fire, Cora spoke up. "In case anybody remembers, we were going to discuss plans for the Spring Carnival with an eye to box-office receipts. How about it, Madam President?" She looked across the orange embers to Holly.

"Brice and I have been talking it over," Holly said, "and all we've been able to come up with are the same old ideas: fish ponds, fortune-telling booths, ring toss." Brice was vice-president of the student council. The rest of the picnic group were either members of the council or active in other school clubs. Holly thought with a touch of pride as she glanced around that the group was the very best of Brent High. Her glance lingered on Brice and wavered, seeing the mud stain still on his temple. She tried to imagine Hugh sitting there with them, cudgeling his brains in the interests of the group, and couldn't. All of Hugh's ambitions seemed to be destructive. Except for art. Even then he scoffed at his own pictures.

She kept thinking about Hugh on the way home and then, later, when she was in her room with its candy-stripe wall paper and its maple furniture, its blowing curtains and great, soft bed, she wondered, "What's Hugh's room like?" and remembered with a sense of fear the black, black pits of his eyes staring at her. She forced the image away, replacing it with the trappings of the Spring Carnival— crepe-paper banners, a ceiling studded with balloons, brightly colored booths. The council would meet formally tomorrow and make the final plans. She had been elected council president this year, her last year at Brent. It was part of her luck, she guessed, and once again she was aware of how many good things she had, so many of them obtained with no effort on her part. "I wish the whole world could be lucky," she sighed aloud. "I wish everybody could be like Brice or Cora or Glen."

The Carnival was two nights away and the council members and volunteers had finished looping the cords of crepe paper from the balcony.

"Tomorrow the balloon ceiling," Cora Smith said wearily. "We ought to get paid for overtime."

Holly laughed and grimaced. "All for good old Brent High. We'll enlist the boys for the balloon work."

"It looks beautiful already," Wilma Rice spoke up.

Holly nodded. The red-and-gold loops, interspersed with paper clowns that she herself had labored over in her little nook of a studio at home, were gay and inviting. She rubbed her tired arms and asked Kay French, "Are we supposed to lock up, or is the janitor?"

"The janitor," Kay said. "As far as I know."

As Holly and Cora left the building, Holly said: "I've been thinking about something. In art class last week we were supposed to make posters advertising something to do with spring. Hugh Kittleson did one on the Spring Carnival. Should we ask him to let us use it on the bulletin board? It's really very good."

Cora shrugged. "I suppose it would be all right. Only, are you sure he doesn't have a bomb concealed in it?"

"A poster ought to be safe enough. I suggested

the idea to Brice and Dave, and they thought it was O. K."

"Well, why the hesitation then?"

Holly shook her head and laughed. "I don't know. If it were anybody else, I wouldn't even think twice. It's only that he—I've hardly ever spoken two whole words to him in my life."

She had not even said "hi" to him in the halls since the incident of the water gun. It seemed better—safer—just not to see Hugh striding down the halls. It wouldn't be easy to go and ask him anything. But she would—in the morning, after art class.

When she got to school the next morning, Brice met her outside home room. "Has Cora told you?" he asked, and his face was pale with anger.

"Told me what?"

"Come on." He took her elbow and propelled her toward the gym.

She stared, unbelieving. "Oh, no! Who—?"

"Do you have to ask?" Brice said. "Kittleson and Company."

"But why?" she breathed, staring at the torn banners and the chalk marks and the litter. "Why—how could anybody be so mean?" Several mocking signs had been tacked up: THE SMART SET THINKS IT'S SMART—AIN'T IT FUN TO BE

TOP DOG?—THE STUDENT COUNCIL RUNS
BRENT.

"The superintendent is mad as hops," Brice said.
"This time Hugh's gone too far."

"Maybe it isn't Hugh," she said weakly. "I could
cry—all the work the girls put in. Now there'll
scarcely be time to patch it up and do the
rest." Real anger flowed through her now where
the numb shock had been. "I was going to talk to
Hugh after class. Well, I'm not going to wait. I'm
going to talk to him right now!"

"I'll go with you—" Brice began, but she was already on her way down the stairs. She had observed
Hugh storing his drawing board in the basement
locker many times. She rounded a corner and saw
him. He was leaning against the wall by the foun-
tain, his hands in his pockets, a superior look on his
face. She hesitated, then strode up to him.

"I—want to ask you something," she stammered.

He raised one dark eyebrow; otherwise, his face
did not move. "Are you sure?"

"Yes." She was suddenly sure. Very sure. "Why
did you and your friends break into the gym and
tear down all—" Her voice broke and she was
furious at herself. She mustn't, she couldn't, break
down in front of this boy. That's what he wanted,
probably—tears "—tear down all we worked so
hard to put up?" Her eyes stung. "It was just plain

mean, Hugh Kittleson. And I was going to ask you to lend us your poster!"

"What poster?" he said, as if he didn't know. But there was movement in his face now. Shock? A sneer?

She swallowed. "The Carnival poster. It was—" the word pushed its way through her anger "—good."

"Oh," he said. His hands fumbled in his faded pockets. She waited for the sharp or insulting remark. It didn't come. And suddenly his eyes didn't look so black and narrow and biting. They were just ordinary dark eyes, and the hard mask had changed to an ordinary face—maybe a bit better than ordinary. He turned awkwardly, almost knocking against her. "You can use it if you want to," he flung over his shoulder.

She had an impulse to run after him, but she didn't have any more to say. He hadn't admitted that he and his gang had been the culprits. But he hadn't denied it either. She wondered if Superintendent Grange would find out. Not that that would help to repair the damage or finish the rest of the work. The bell rang, and she rushed to her own locker for her books.

She couldn't concentrate on her class. She kept thinking about Hugh. Funny how she had been so furious and meant to say every hurting thing she could and then had come up with that business about the poster instead! And what was even more peculiar was the way he had acted—embarrassed, almost as if he were shy and didn't know what to say or do. She propped her chin on her hand and wondered. By the time the class was over, she had a radical idea, so radical that she wondered if she were really in her right mind.

She went first to Mr. Kerrit, the council's adviser, and asked him to have an announcement made over the intercommunication system asking for more volunteers to help finish decorating the gym. Then she went in pursuit of Hugh again.

He was in the art room, hunched over the wide, yellow drawing board, his pencil clutched in one hand. He glanced up when she came in, and a dark, slow red spread over his cheekbones. He reached down beside the desk and pulled the Carnival poster from its portfolio. "Here," he blurted, pushing the poster at her. He crouched quickly over the drawing board again, his shoulders high and tense as if he were braced against an expected blow.

She stood holding the poster nervously, not knowing quite how to say what she wanted to say. It had seemed a brilliant idea before, but now she was uncertain.

"I would have offered it myself," Hugh mumbled, staring straight at the blank drawing board, "only—I didn't think you people would want it."

You people! The phrase stung her. As if she and Brice and the others were a separate class! She thought back over her three years at Brent. Hugh and his gang never came to the parties; they never joined in club activities; they didn't share in the school spirit; and they probably never even bothered to vote in the elections. Maybe it had been that way with them since kindergarten. They had got left out, or pushed out, and now they stayed outside deliberately and jeered.

"Hugh," she began, trying to make it as casual as if she were asking Cora or Glen, "we could use your help—and the help of your friends—in decorating the gym after school." She rushed on quickly, her own face burning. "There are over a hundred balloons to be blown up and tied and hung —and new banners."

His forehead creased and his lips parted. "Me?" The wise, mocking look returned. "What's the gag?"

"I just thought you might like to."

He frowned, puzzled again and taken off guard. "Oh." He scribbled meaninglessly on the white drawing paper. "Even if I did want to, I couldn't. Grange wouldn't let me. He knows that I was the one who broke into the gym last night."

"You *told* him?"

"D'you think I'm slap-happy?" He tried to sneer, but there was something embarrassed and self-conscious about it that made Holly suspect that he *had* confessed to the superintendent. His next words gave him away. "He'd have found out, anyhow. You people would have seen to that!"

Holly pushed back the little fork of anger that prodded her. "I wouldn't have. Brice wouldn't. None of the others either."

"Oh, no?" There was a flicker of uncertainty in his voice. He hesitated, then shrugged and pretended to yawn. "Well, I'll probably be expelled, anyhow."

"There's probation," she said. "If the council backed you up—"

"Fat chance!"

"I'm on the council."

He was silent, and the two red spots on his cheekbones glowed brighter. His pencil dug almost viciously into the drawing board. "So what? You're no different from the others. I'm not going to kid myself about that."

There was a sharp rap, and Holly turned to see Miss Callister tapping on the exhibit board for attention. Holly hadn't even heard the bell ring for class! But she had to settle this with Hugh. "Please,

Hugh," she coaxed, "come and help us just this once."

Everyone was staring at them now. Someone giggled. She saw Hugh's jaw stiffen. He picked up his brush and made invisible strokes on the paper. "Blow your own balloons."

Holly turned away, defeated, her cheeks flaming. At her own desk she got out her art materials without knowing what she was doing. She had acted like a fool. She should have known better than to try to do anything with a boy like Hugh. He probably got a big kick out of humiliating her. Maybe he even thought she was running after him, as some of the class members seemed to think, judging by their silly stares. She tacked paper onto her drawing board angrily. Hugh's poster leaned beside her desk. She was going to put that up on the bulletin board in spite of his rudeness. It was a good poster and the Carnival Committee needed it.

"If everybody at school would pitch in, we'd get somewhere at this business," Cora sighed as she hung another balloon from the balcony ceiling.

"Everybody's a big word," Brice said as he steadied a ladder for Holly. "There're always a few people, everywhere, who never take responsibility."

Holly pulled off a withered balloon and tossed

it to Brice. "Well, maybe they don't have responsibility offered to them." She frowned thoughtfully.
"Or maybe not in the right way." Her sigh was even
deeper than Cora's. "That's what I thought once,
anyhow. Now I just don't know."

Brice was staring past her. His jaw sagged.
"Well, for Pete's sake! Get a look at what's coming
in the side door!" He began rolling up his sleeves,
his face grim. "This time we're ready for our
friends. It's time Mr. Hugh Kittleson and his gang
learned a lesson." He strode forward, his fists tight.

"Wait!" Holly ran after him and put a restrain-
ing hand on his arm.

It was Hugh and his group all right—Corky and
Pink and Jimmy and five others. But they weren't
storming in like boys intent on trouble. They
drifted in quietly, almost sheepishly. When they
were all inside the door, they stopped and just stood
there as if they didn't know what to do next.

"Come on, Brice," Holly whispered, and, seizing
his hand, she pulled him along with her across the
gym floor. "Hi," she sang out as soon as she was
near enough to the stiff cluster of boys. "It's a good
thing you got here! We're about bushed. Where
do you want to start?" Hugh advanced a step beyond the others, and Holly addressed him directly.
"How about making some new clowns, Hugh? The

ones I did are pretty corny." She met his dark eyes hopefully, holding her breath.

Hugh's eyes were the first to drop. Then, slowly, he glanced up at the paper clown dangling over his head. "They look O. K. to me. What's wrong with 'em?" But he didn't wait for an answer. He turned to his companions. "Jim, you help Brice here with whatever he's doing. Corky, you go ask some of the others what they want help with. Don't stand there like lunks. We didn't come here to rest, you know." Hugh's words were tough, on the outside. Holly smothered a smile. She knew he didn't want his followers to think he was going soft all of a sudden.

His henchmen scattered, and Brice went with them. Hugh scowled at Holly. "Well, where's your paper and scissors? Let's get started, if we're going to make clowns."

"They're over here on the table," Holly said meekly and let him stride ahead of her across the room.

✿✿✿✿✿✿✿✿✿✿✿✿✿✿✿✿✿✿✿✿✿✿✿

Amber Girl

by ELIZABETH EICHER

Amber Girl

by ELIZABETH EICHER

Mr. Digby's letter arrived while Mother and Dad were on their vacation—which was certainly not *my* fault. But I was blamed for everything just the same. Mr. Digby blamed me; Mr. Perkins, Ellen's father, blamed me; and even Dad said that if I had *any* sense—

Ellen and I had walked over to my house after breakfast to pick up the mail. It looked like the start of a peaceful summer. Peaceful—ha!

We sat down on the steps. "Circulars, bills, magazines. 'Miss Judy Juniper'—that's me!"

"Let's see." Ellen leaned closer. "Well, who's it from?"

I looked at the postmark. "Digby's Station," I exclaimed. "Why, it's from Mr. Digby!" I tore open the envelope and shrieked. "Ellen! He's sending

179

it! For me! Isn't that wonderful?" I hugged her, the mail cascading down onto the grass.

"Judy!" Ellen gasped for breath. "Who's sending what?"

"Mr. Digby," I said, "my grandfather, is sending me a present. A dog. Amber Girl. I'll read it to you. 'Dear Judy, I'm finally in a position to keep my promise of sending you a present. Be good to Amber Girl. Mr. Digby.' There!"

"Your grandfather? He doesn't sound like a grandfather, signing himself Mr. Digby."

"Well, he is though. He just doesn't like to be called 'Grandfather.' He promised to send me one of the next puppies. He raises cocker spaniels and horses. Think of it, Ellen! A cocker spaniel for my own! It's golden too—it will have to be, with a name like Amber Girl."

"You're lucky," Ellen sighed. "Dad won't let me have a dog."

"He won't mind Amber Girl, will he?" I asked anxiously. "It's only until Mother and Dad come home."

"I guess not," Ellen said. "We'll ask him."

We couldn't ask Mr. Perkins until lunch time. "Mr. Perkins," I said, "my grandfather is sending me a present and you don't mind if I keep it here, do you? Just until Mother and Dad come home?"

"And what is he sending you?" he asked.

"Amber Girl," I said. "She's only a puppy."

His face lengthened. "Puppy?" he repeated. "H'm. Well—"

"It probably won't come for days," I said.

Mr. Perkins brightened. "That's so. Well, all right, Judy." He turned to Ellen. "Only don't get ideas. This is an exception."

"Thanks, Mr. Perkins," I said. "I promise you won't know there's a dog around."

I guess trains run faster than we figured. The very next day the express agent phoned me. "Judy Juniper?" he almost shouted. "There's an animal down here for you."

"Thanks," I said. "I'll be right down and pick her up."

"Think you can manage it?" he asked dubiously.

"Of course." I was scornful. "I know all about Amber Girl."

"Who?"

"Amber Girl. Never mind. I'll be right down."

"O.K.," he said. "Be mighty glad to see you."

I hung up. "It's Amber Girl. She's there. That stupid agent—thinking I couldn't manage a puppy!"

"We ought to have a leash, I guess," Ellen said practically.

Naturally we didn't have one, but I found a

length of rope and an old belt I thought might do. We went straight to the office.

"I've come for Amber Girl," I said. "I'm Judy Juniper. You can bring her out here."

"Oh, I can, can I?" He just looked at me. "Just like that. Bring her here, she says."

A horrible thought occurred to me. "There—isn't any money due on her, is there?"

"No."

"Well, I'm here," I said.

"You better go out there to the rear—pick her up there. How are you going to get her home? Ride her?"

"Don't be ridiculous," I said. He was just trying to be funny.

"O.K.," he said. "You can go through that door there." We followed him. "Hey, Ed!" he almost bawled. "These kids have come for the livestock."

We walked through a huge warehouse, then out into the bright sunshine, "Well," I said, "where's the—"

At that moment there was an awful noise right behind me. I shrieked and whirled, and shrieked again. The biggest horse I'd ever seen was practically biting my ear off.

"Ow!" I yelled. Scaring me like that. It wasn't funny. I looked around. "Where's Amber Girl?"

"There."

"Where?"

"There. Behind you."

Slowly I turned, as though my blood was congealing. The horse. There wasn't another live animal in sight. "Oh, no!" I moaned. "A horse?"

"Sure looks like one."

"There's some mistake," I mumbled. "It's a dog. What I'm to get, I mean."

He inspected the papers in his hand. "One horse to Miss Judy Juniper. She's all yours."

I gulped.

"Well, take her away."

"Me?" I squeaked. "Me?"

"Came down for that purpose, didn't you?"

"But—it was supposed to be a dog—" Mr. Digby hadn't really said "dog," though. He'd said "Amber Girl." So this big brown animal was Amber Girl. Maybe he *had* once promised me a horse, but I couldn't remember it.

The man took the rope from my limp hand and put it around the horse's neck. "Here you are."

"But what'll I *do* with it?"

"Girl, I got enough worries of my own. Lead her out through that gate." He walked away.

I looked at Ellen. Her eyes were still big blue saucers. "I—I guess I have to take her to your house," I said. "My house—we don't have any yard."

"I don't think my father's going to like it," Ellen said, which proved a masterpiece of understatement.

"But he promised."

"I know, but—"

I knew, myself. Mr. Perkins had consented to harboring one small dog. But Amber Girl? She was rolling her eyes wildly, snorting, and making all sorts of scary noises.

"I can't leave her here, Ellen. You heard what the man said. It won't be but seven days."

"Well—"

The horse gave a loud whinny, and I jumped a foot. "Come on, Amber Girl, come on."

Amber Girl didn't seem to recognize her name, but followed when I tugged at the rope. We went slowly down Main Street, with everyone watching us.

Ellen eyed Amber Girl. "I'll walk on the sidewalk, Judy. Maybe she'll be calmer if there aren't two of us."

"O.K.," I said.

When we got back to the house, Ellen's mother and father were gone. We tied Amber Girl to the clothesline, and I got her a bucket of water. In five minutes she'd trampled all over Mrs. Perkins' iris bed, and cut big horseshoe gobs of turf from the yard.

Their next-door neighbor spied Amber Girl and gave a little shriek. "Ellen! Not a horse!"

"Yes, Mrs. Moore," Ellen said. "It's Judy's, though."

Mrs. Moore stared. "What is your father going to say, Ellen? I'd get that horse out of there fast if I were you."

Ellen looked worried. "See, Judy?"

"But I can't. I haven't any place to keep her."

"Where will you keep her when your parents come home?"

"I don't know," I admitted. Our yard is hardly big enough for a good-sized dog, to say nothing of a horse.

"Maybe," Ellen said slowly, "you'd better send it back."

"Send back Amber Girl? Ellen, are you mad? You can't send a present back."

"But if you've no place to keep it—"

"I'd better write Mr. Digby right away and thank him," I said.

I worked hard on the letter, and it was a good one: "Dear Mr. Digby," I wrote. "Amber Girl has arrived, and she is the most beautiful present a girl ever had. I'm all excited. You couldn't have surprised me more. Thanks ever so much. Amber Girl is exactly what I wanted." I read that last sentence over and crossed it out. That was going a little too far. I copied the letter and went out to look at Amber Girl again. She was cropping the grass.

"Food!" I exclaimed. "Ellen, we've forgotten all about feeding Amber Girl. You hunt up a bucket or something."

"What will we put in the bucket?"

"Oh, anything that horses eat."

"Judy, *I* don't know anything about horses. I never even rode a pony," Ellen confessed.

"Well," I said, swallowing hard, "I don't know much. Apples, and oats, and sugar, I guess." We found some apples, and I took a fistful of loaf sugar.

"I guess if she's hungry, she'll eat anything," Ellen said morosely, and dumped a half box of rolled oats into the pail.

I wasn't too happy about feeding her, but I couldn't let on. She gobbled up everything and still seemed hungry.

"Tomorrow," I said, "we'll call up the feed store."

"Tomorrow?" Ellen said halfheartedly, staring at the churned up yard.

"It'll grow back," I assured her. "Anyway, it's just until Mother and Dad come home, Ellen."

We had a little trouble with Ellen's mother when she came home. She flatly refused to go out the back door, and Ellen and I had to carry out the garbage.

"The idea—a horse in our yard!" she scolded. "I ask you!"

I was relieved when Mr. Perkins called to say that he would be late in coming home. But I rejoiced too soon. We were just starting to get ready for bed when a horrible cry startled us.

"What *is* it, Ellen?" I moaned.

Just then Amber Girl whinnied.

"Oh, it's only the horse!" I exclaimed, and flopped on the bed.

There was a sudden clatter beneath our window, and the back door slammed.

"She's coming in!" Ellen cried. "Judy, your horse came in the house!"

"She couldn't! She—" I was interrupted by a roar. "It's your father," I said, and we rushed down.

There was a big hole over his right knee where he'd torn his suit, and earth was smeared all over the front of his shirt. Amber Girl, it seemed, had come up behind him and stuck her head over his shoulder. She had scared him so, he'd fallen down and lost his glasses—which Amber Girl found with her foot.

"Who . . . where . . . what?" Before he let us go to bed he issued an ultimatum: before tomorrow night we *had* to get rid of Amber Girl. "I don't care *who* Mr. Digby is, or *whose* horse it is," he roared, "that horse has got to go!"

Breakfast was anything but cheerful. Mr. Perkins limped because of his sore knee. He squinted because of his missing glasses. I was thankful that, after barking, "Good morning," he never said another word, but stalked out of the house.

Mrs. Perkins' lips were set in a straight line. "Soon as you girls finish the dishes, you must get that horse out of here."

"Yes, ma'am," I said, and Ellen and I slunk out.

"Are you going to take her to your house?"

"Don't be silly. I've got a better idea. We'll take her to the zoo. They've got lots of cages and enclosures."

Ellen sighed. "That's a good idea. Only, it's two miles to the zoo and we are both afraid to ride Amber Girl."

It was a long two miles. My feet were sore, and my arms ached trying to hold tightly to Amber Girl's rope. She kept tossing her head and dancing around. When we arrived at the zoo, the gates were locked.

"Doesn't open until ten," the guard said.

"But we're not visitors," I said. "We've brought an animal."

He frowned. "Well, O.K. I'll open up for you." He called the manager.

"Well, you young ladies have something to donate to the zoo?" he asked. He spied Amber Girl. "A horse!"

"Yes, sir," I said. "Only we're not *donating* her."

"But you don't understand. I can't use zoo funds to buy a horse. We have to purchase rare birds and animals—not domesticated animals like horses."

"Oh, I'm not *selling* her!" I exclaimed. "I couldn't do that—not Mr. Digby's present."

"Then what is it you *do* want?" he asked.

"Just to leave her here until Mother and Dad come home." I explained all about Mr. Perkins and everything. When I'd finished, he took out his handkerchief and wiped his forehead.

"You don't understand," he said. "It's true that we take in little animals sometimes, that people give us, just so they won't starve. But as a free boarding home for horses—young lady, I'd have every tax-payer in the city on my neck."

"You won't take her?" I mumbled, aghast.

"Absolutely not. You find a boarding stable—there's the place for you." He went in and closed the door.

"Well," I said. We still had Amber Girl, and we had two miles to walk back home.

Mr. Perkins was on the porch when we finally arrived. His face turned dark red, as though he were going to explode, when he saw us. "Call a stable right this minute," he growled.

The people were really very difficult to deal with. "You'll have to pay the board in advance," the man said.

I gulped, and covered the mouthpiece. "He has to be paid in advance," I reported. "All I have is my allowance—"

Mr. Perkins swallowed hard. "I'll pay it," he said. "Tell them to come with a horse trailer right away."

I did. "They say that will be five dollars extra," I reported.

He glared at the ceiling and groaned. "All right. Five dollars. And be prompt about it."

We sat out on the porch in silence. When the truck and trailer drove up, Mr. Perkins counted out the bills as though it hurt him. He muttered something and then said, "Thank goodness!" when the trailer with Amber Girl bounced out of sight. We went into the house.

"There's a long-distance call for you, Judy," Mrs. Perkins said. "Call operator three."

The wires hummed, then a loud, "Hello."

"Dad?" I asked. "Oh, Mr. Digby!"

"Judy," he cried. He seemed to be excited. "Judy, have you got Digby's Daughter?"

"Oh, no, I've got Amber Girl, and I—"

He interrupted me. "You *can't* have Amber Girl! That dog's in California!"

"D—did you say 'dog'?"

"Of course I said 'dog!' "

"But—but I've got a *horse!*"

"*You've* got Digby's Daughter? Why didn't you say so? Why didn't you wire? Here that dumb stable hand of mine sent the pup to Far Acre Farms in California, and sent the horse that Far Acre bought to you! Switched the addresses. Why didn't you tell me?"

"But—"

"The idea, keeping a fine horse like Digby's Daughter and saying nothing about it! Judy, what's the matter with you?"

"But Mr. Digby—"

"Now, you listen to me. You ship that horse back here right this minute. Understand?"

"Yes, Mr. Digby, but—"

"No buts now. A girl your age! You ship her right back. You hear?"

"Yes, Mr. Digby."

Slowly I hung up and turned to face the Perkinses. "I have to ship Amber Girl—the horse, I mean—back. It was all a mistake."

"Are you telling me!" said Mr. Perkins. "This whole thing's a mistake."

So Mr. Perkins had to advance the shipping charges. When Mother and Dad came home and

Dad saw the bill! They all blamed me, as if I could help it that Amber Girl and Digby's Daughter got switched. Oh, yes—Amber Girl, the real one, is coming tomorrow.